Mr. M's Notebook:

Memorial High

A Teacher's Life

A Trilogy
By John Splaine

Mr. M's Notebook
Book Three: Memorial High

This is a work of fiction. The characters depicted in this novel are not associated with any person living or deceased. Any resemblance is unintended and coincidental. The events, except those that can be verified as historically accurate, did not happen.

Published by Piscataqua Press
An imprint of RiverRun Bookstore
32 Daniel Street | Portsmouth NH | 03801
www.riverrunbookstore.com
www.piscataquapress.com

ISBN: 978-1-950381-83-8
Printed in the United States of America.

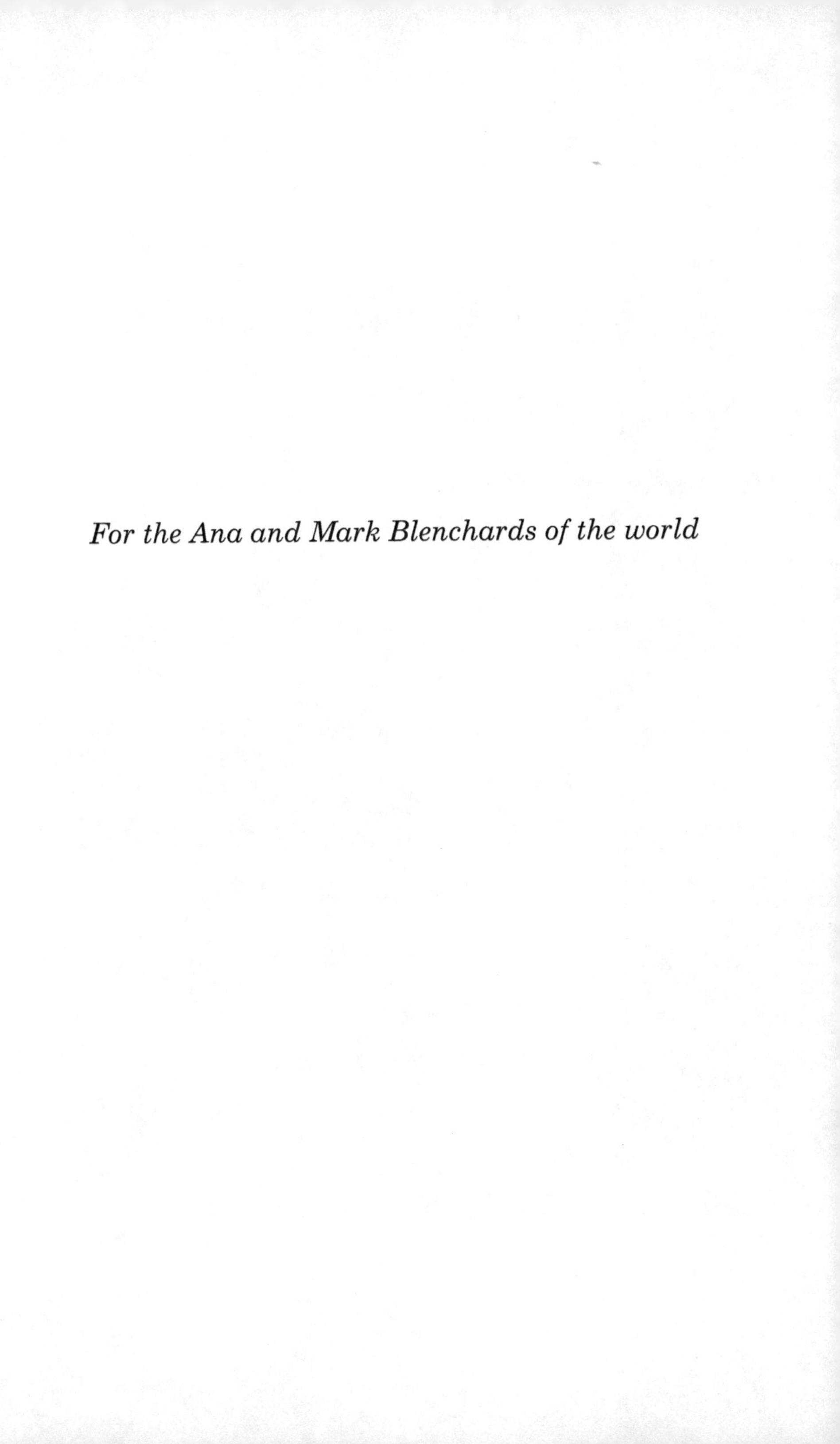

For the Ana and Mark Blenchards of the world

Table of Contents

Chapter 1: 9/11

September summons:
Shadows stretch.
Daylight retreats.
Nature exhales.
Plants morph.
Trees repose.
Deciduous sheds.
Sprigs sprout.
Foliage tumbles.
Winds muster.
Leaves blow.
Ferns run.
Grass fevers.
Pollen snows.
Chlorophyll blends.
Pigments burgeon.
Hues paint.
Tints flourish.
Saplings seep.
Slumber deepens.
Babies climb.
School bells ring.
Teachers enlighten.

Poetry inspires.
Learners blossom.
Classrooms awaken.

Ana and I sipped coffee on the Tuesday of the first full week of school in the fall semester of 2001. On this September morning, we expressed to each other how beautiful and peaceful the day dawned.

My name is Mark Blenchard. Since the fall semester of 1970, I have taught at Bailey T. S. Memorial High School. I am known throughout the school community as "Mr. M." Ana has taught in Gorham Center Elementary since 1973. We have been husband and wife since 1970.

On the morning of September 11, 2001, our friend, Wanda Brade, was scheduled to fly from Boston to New York. We wished her well in a phone call the night before her departure.

Wanda had arranged a visit with relatives in the United States' largest city. Tuesday's blue, clear sky meant there would be no weather delays at the airport.

In June of 2001, Ana and I had attended a college graduation for one of my former students. At the ceremony, I said to Ana, "The entire world awaits these joyful graduates. They have a bright future ahead of them."

Gentle warm breezes foretelling summer balminess bathed families and friends as the scholars accepted diplomas on a cloudless June day. The baccalaureates' hopes and dreams swirled through the audience.

Ana and I wondered what my student's world would be as she asked for both of us, "What challenges will this generation encounter?"

On that sun-drenched commencement day, peace and prosperity stirred and animated the celebration. The attendees envisioned endless opportunities for America's students, our families, and ourselves.

Wanda Brade, our friend flying to New York City on September 11, 2001, also cherished the possibilities in front of her—possibilities she never got to fulfill.

Little did any of us foresee that as the new century unfolded, the world-churning events on the eleventh day in September—in the year two thousand and one—would change everything.

Late for class, Evelyn Price sprinted into my classroom in Bailey T. S. Memorial High School in Gorham, Massachusetts. Evelyn was characteristically tardy, so her dash into room 202 on this September eleventh morning did not surprise me or her classmates.

Out of breath, she stammered, "Mr. M. have you heard what is happening in New York?"

"No, I haven't," I responded. "What are you talking about Evelyn?"

As Evelyn caught her breath, I asked, "What did happen?"

"Well, Mr. M., I heard that an airplane crashed into one of the World Trade Center's towers."

"What?" I exclaimed.

Another student raced frantically into the room as the ninth hour of September's eleventh day in 2001 approached. "Airplanes have crashed into both of the World Trade Center's buildings, Mr. M." Juan said.

"Juan, are you sure?" I asked.

"Yes, Mr. M. First, one plane—then another. There are also reports a plane hit a building in Washington, D. C. Turn on the television, Mr. M., and you will see for yourself what is happening."

I turned the classroom set on.

We all watched. My students' fear-filled, tear-drenched faces revealed their concern for family living and working in and around New York City and Washington, D. C. Student angst reflected the apprehension their teachers felt.

As school buses lined for early-dismissal, I thought of Wanda flying to New York. I did not sleep much the night of September 11, 2001.

I summoned the social studies and history department faculty for a meeting on the twelfth day of the ninth month in the first full year of the twenty-first century. We knew the world had changed on the day before—we had changed too.

I dropped my cautious nature as I spoke. "Lesson plans about the events of yesterday are not in the approved curriculum, and we have had little preparation time for what we should teach about the attacks. However, I believe as educators we have an obligation to help our students and ourselves through this. Since the start of World War II and the attack on Pearl Harbor, we have not been attacked like this on United States soil."

I continued, "This is new for all of us. As history teaches us, from 1914 to 1918 in the first of the world wars, nations entangled in alliances spread devastation through large portions of the planet. Just two decades later, a second world war threatened earth's civilized societies. More recently, as the children of the Cold War we have lived with the possibility of nuclear weapons radiating the globe. Yesterday, terror assaulted the United States."

"Mark, you can't stop trying to teach and sometimes preach to us, can you?" Lacey Walsh said to nervous laughter.

"I realize I go overboard sometimes, and I may have this time although I don't think so. However, your response Lacey has helped break my tension—at least momentarily."

"Mine too, but like yours—just for the moment," Lacey said.

"To go on, though, the world is in this together," I said. "Our planet is the only one we have—no more denials. As educators, we must teach about what this attack on the United States means now and in the future. We have been teaching in our classes about Orwell's 1984 and Huxley's *Brave New World* dystopias. The visions have merged in September eleventh's events. Here we are with a possible conflagration staring us in the face. What are we to do in our classrooms now?" I asked.

"Your comments are frightening me, Mark—using words like 'conflagration.' Are you being too extreme about this?" Karla Betts asked.

"I hope he is," Jake Spanner said. "But I don't think Mark would have said what he has if he didn't perceive the threat to our country and the world."

Ana and I hastily invited the Friday potluck group to our home on September 14, 2001. The topic for this evening's discussion was immediate—it had been chosen for us.

During our times together over the years, we had discussed our work as educators as well as news events in the greater society. Participants in the regular potluck dinner group included Cheryl Wattsen, English teacher, and chair of the department in Bailey High School; Bailey High art teacher, Karla Betts; Gorham Central Elementary School teacher, April Danniels; Bailey High social studies and media literacy teacher, Lacey Walsh; and Bailey High social studies teachers, John Browne, Charles Yates, Jake Spanner, Zack Barber, and Angela Tremonte, who replaced Megan Straffa as a regular member of the potluck. Ana and I completed the gathering, and we continued to host the discussion. We sometimes invited guests to join us, but not on this evening.

I started our discussion, "The assaults on New York's

twin towers, the attack on the Pentagon in Washington, and the downing of a plane in Pennsylvania headed for the United States Capitol—these calamities have shocked us all and altered our outlook on the world forever."

Cheryl Wattsen interrupted, "Mark, first, I believe, before we draw any conclusions, we need to understand what and who struck us on September eleventh and why it happened."

"And, Mark, to add to Cheryl's comment let me add a question I have been thinking about." Charles Yates said. "As we go through the school year and after, how are we going to teach about what transpired on Tuesday? Our students are living in a 'brave new world'—the attacks have seen to that. In this age of terror, the students are alarmed and terrified for the future. Frankly, so am I."

Charles continued, "Though afraid of what is to come, I am not sure the students realize and understand how much has changed in the short time since the attacks. In fact, I am not sure individual faculty understand the magnitude of what happened on September eleventh or the prospective aftermath. I know I don't."

"Keep going, Charles. You are making sense. I think that if she were here, even Megan Straffa would agree," Jake Spanner said.

"Thanks, Jake. That is high praise coming from a liberal, although I am not sure Megan would ever agree with anything I said," Charles quipped.

"You are welcome for my comments anyway," Jake said with a smile. "I am just trying to relieve the tension, and Megan would appreciate that."

"I understand. However, this is serious stuff." Charles said. "As a result of what I have observed in my classes since Tuesday, it is clear to me that only a few of my students can handle the possibility of a future filled with the kind of danger we are witnessing. Many of my students are petrified when they think of leaving the relatively safe confines of Gorham. Several expressed they do not think they are or will be safe anywhere, whether it is here or elsewhere. I agree with them. The world ahead of them and us is filled with threats and uncertainty."

"Thank you, Charles. I appreciate the points you are making," Cheryl said.

"Mark, I want to go back to the other question you started with: Who would do something like this to our country?" Lacey Walsh asked.

"I do not know," I said.

"It is obviously terrorists from somewhere," Zack Barber asserted.

"From where, Zack?" I asked.

"I don't know. If I guessed, it would be mere speculation at this point on my part," Zack said.

"Hey everyone, if we don't know who attacked us, then we obviously don't have any idea why we were struck," Jake said.

"I don't know the answer to that either, but merely speculating doesn't help. As a nation, we could be wrong about the perpetrators and risk retaliating against innocents. That would make things worse—much worse," Zack said.

"How could someone hate us that much to attack us the way they did?" Karla Betts asked. "Why do you think they do, Charles?"

"I believe they hate us because of our freedom," Charles responded.

"I don't think that is it at all, Charles," Jake said.

"What do you think the motivation is then, Jake?" Charles asked.

"Charles, I believe it is because they believe that we

want their oil and their land—they want us to get off their lands—especially their Holy Lands," Jake said.

"Regardless the motives Charles and Jake have mentioned, the fact is that an onslaught occurred. What should our country do, Mr. M.?" Lacey asked.

"I don't know, Lacey. What do the rest of you think?" I asked.

"The United States should go get them and capture the culprits whoever they are, and then put them on trial which would be more than they did for our citizens who were killed on September eleventh," Charles said.

"The problem is, Charles, who are THEY?" John Browne asked.

"I believe it is Saddam Hussein and his allies," Charles stated.

"Charles, how do we know it was him and that he ordered the attack?" John asked.

"John, he hates us. People like him despise us. They despise us because of our freedom. We know that—don't we?" Charles said.

"Maybe, but I would certainly like more evidence about who exactly is involved," John said.

"John, do you doubt it was him?" Charles asked.

"I am just not as certain as you are about such things, Charles. I need the proof before I arrive at a conclusion," John said.

"And, Charles, just because Saddam Hussein does not like us, that doesn't mean he is responsible for 9/11—does it?" Zack asked.

"It is more than he just doesn't like us. He has grievances against us and other Western nations. So, yes, I believe he is the perpetrator. In fact, Zack, in Hussein's case, he has expressed a lot stronger mindset than 'Saddam Hussein does not like us.' I think I am quoting you accurately. I believe his attitude toward us, Zack, is a whole lot stronger than he just does not like us. I am convinced he loathes us and everything we stand for. I believe he will do whatever he thinks is necessary to destroy us," Charles said.

"I understand Charles. I get your point. It is clear to me after tonight's discussion that we have a lot of work to do in our classrooms. Currently, we do not know much. Besides, in this discussion so far we have been all over the place," Jake said.

"I agree Jake. We do not know much right now. We lack information on who attacked us and why. The United States should not do anything militarily until we know more. As a country, we have to get this right," I said.

After the group departed for the evening, Ana said to me, "As educators we need to avoid the trap of jumping to conclusions. If our government overreacts and attacks or invades the wrong country—we could be in a war without end."

"Ana, I agree with you. Terror as warfare could last for decades. If that happens, to say the least, it is not a positive outlook for those of us in Gorham, in the United States, or around the world," I said.

"On the other hand, Mark, teachers going into classrooms imparting doom and gloom messages about the world will distress and upset our students rather than inform them," Ana said.

"Okay, Honey, I hear you. However, when we return to our students on Monday, what should we do and say? We must do and say something. Don't we?" I asked.

"I do not know what we should do. This whole thing is so upsetting. The attack on the United States on September eleventh has implications for our country and the world. I don't even know what to say to our own children, never mind knowing what we should do next as a country, or what to do in our classrooms when school resumes next week," Ana said.

"The reality is we have to teach on Monday. So, Ana, what do we say and do?" I asked.

"I don't know, Mark. I just don't know."

Chapter 2: Crash

I had not heard from Derek Randallston since he left Bailey T. S. Memorial High School in April of 1975. I wondered what his life was like after the Gorham, Massachusetts, school system summarily dismissed him for an allegation involving a student.

I decided to search the Internet to find out where Derek is and what he is doing. Because of fear of what I might discover, I had previously been reluctant to locate him. My lack of courage in standing up for Derek when his job was in jeopardy continues to haunt me—I had failed to support Mr. D. when he most needed me to do so.

Fear also had halted me when Ken Lewiston died of AIDS in 1985. Dreading social opprobrium, I did not speak for him at his memorial service. I am still developing the strength to advocate for and do what I know to be right.

Decades have passed since I last had contact with Derek, so I thought it was time for me to communicate with him. I needed closure and maybe he did too. I typed his name into a search engine.

What I found shook me. A news item from a website in Los Angeles reported that a Derek A. Randallston had died in an automobile accident. The account of the collision indicated alcohol had been involved.

I looked for and found an obituary. The announcement of the death listed teaching at Bailey High as his first employment. I knew I had found the right Derek A. Randallston.

I wrote to the address recorded in the obituary to express my condolences.

In return, Diane Randallston, identified as Derek's daughter, responded:

"Dear Mr. Blenchard:

"Thank you for your expression of sorrow upon hearing of my father's passing. Until I heard from you, I did not know anything significant about my dad as a teacher. I had always wondered why he never talked about his first job. I knew he had been a teacher in Massachusetts, but other than what I put into the announcement of my dad's death, I did not know much about his work in education. So, thank you for that information.

"I hope I can find out from you what my father taught and something about his teaching methods. I would also like to know what led to his leaving his job in Bailey High School. Other than the fact he taught in a high school, my father never said anything to me about the teaching position or why he left it.

"I do know that what he did do and what happened were important to him, so much so that he kept his experience in Gorham, Massachusetts, close to him. I would have wanted to know more, but he never talked about it and I did not broach the subject. Something about the job and his leaving it affected him deeply.

"After I received your letter, I began looking through my father's filing cabinet marked 'personal.' I had previously hesitated looking into his personal files. I guess I was afraid of what I might find.

"In a folder marked, 'Bailey High,' I found a letter addressed to you. I am assuming it was never sent and you never received it. My father's letter looks like the original and lacks a signature.

"I have printed below the exact contents of the letter meant for you.

'Dear Mark:

'It has been over twenty-five years since I left Bailey T. S. Memorial High School behind me. I need to say, however, that I have missed teaching so very much. The classroom has never left me, and I have never left it. I think about teaching every day. Even though I departed Gorham, Massachusetts, on that April 1975 day, my heart has remained in the Bailey High I loved.

'I have been unable emotionally and psychologically to accept the fact I had to vacate the profession I treasured. I have never recovered from losing my teaching job.

'Mark, particularly distressing is my memory of the students I had to abandon. I still dream about teaching in Bailey. Even though it has been almost three decades, I continue to regret having to leave my colleagues and students in Bailey High.

'I am not sure if you have ever heard the true story about Lydia Smith being with me in the car the evening the police came over to the parked car. You may have heard a version of what was happening, but I want to provide you with the facts as I see them.

"The truth is I was trying to help Lydia work through some problems. I tried telling anyone who would listen that Lydia and I were just having a conversation, which is all we were doing.

'Superintendent Mitchell Appletone never gave me a chance to explain the situation. He just fired me. I have never gotten over it.

'After I left Gorham, Massachusetts, behind me in

the spring of 1975, I have looked back daily. Words fail in communicating how trying it was and continues to be for me to lose my teaching job. I cherished the profession and everything about it.

'I floated around for a while—job to job—apartment to apartment. During that time, my biggest mistake—actually, just one of my big mistakes among others—was that I befriended alcohol. I still drink daily and live for the bottle.

'My addiction has brought all kinds of problems—personal and professional. Even if I wanted to, I have not stopped drinking, nor do I believe I could stop. Drink is my refuge. Right now, I do not want to give it up. Along with my daughter, I feel it is all I have.

'I did get married, but it did not last long. It was a contest between my drinking or my marriage—drinking won. A daughter resulted from the marriage. Her name is Diane. I move around frequently, so I have not seen her for over a year. We exchange birthday cards and send each other gifts now and then.

'By the way, my daughter, Diane Randallston, is preparing to become a teacher. I have mentioned your name to her a couple of times. She knows you as Mr. M.

'Sincerely, Derek Randallston'

"Mr. M., the above is what my father intended to send to you, but apparently he never did.

"As I mentioned, Mr. M., my father died in an automobile crash. He was traveling at a high rate of speed when he ran into a concrete road barrier. I do not believe it was an accident—my father intended to die.

"I wish you the best Mr. M. I hope to meet you some day.

"Yours truly, Diane Randallston"

Chapter 3: Ms. D.

"Dear Mr. M.:

"I wrote to you previously about my father and his death. Now, I write to you because I intend to carry on where my dad left off. I hope to live the life he wanted—as a teacher.

"From everything I have heard, my father was an effective and innovative educator. His life ended when he still had good years ahead.

"I want to continue what my dad started by teaching in Bailey T. S. Memorial High School. I aspire to fulfill some of those years for him, for myself, and for the students in the Gorham, Massachusetts, school district. Consequently, I have applied for a teaching position to teach history and social studies.

"I always yearned to be a teacher. For reasons I understand better now, whenever I was with my dad, we role-played teacher-student games. In that sense, he was still a teacher—imparting to me the joy of teaching and learning. He was usually the student—and I the teacher. From a young age, I never thought of doing anything other than teaching and learning."

After we received Diane Randallston's application for an open teaching position in Bailey High, the school system decided to interview her. From the moment we met her, the faculty recognized she understood what she was applying to do and why she chose to teach. With the endorsement of all who met her, it did not take long for the Gorham, Massachusetts school administration to offer Diane a teaching position.

I began meeting regularly for coffee with Diane after she accepted the job to join the Bailey High faculty. In our first session, Diane wanted to discuss what had happened with her father, and to learn more about him as a teacher. Diane said in this initial discussion, "Mr. M., even though he never talked about it specifically, it is clear to me now that my father missed teaching so much that he believed he could not live without working in the profession he loved."

"Diane, what you said about your father and his dedication to life as a teacher has also become increasingly clear to me," I responded. "Your father loved teaching and belonged in the classroom. I just wish that after he lost his job in Bailey High, he could have found something fulfilling so he could have continued living a complete life. Maybe he could have even found a job in education somewhere else."

"Mr. Blenchard, I, too, wish he could have returned to teaching. Are you able to tell me what happened when my father taught here in Gorham and lost his job?"

"Diane, please just call me Mr. M., and the students and faculty will refer to you as Ms. D."

"Sure, Mr. M., I will try to do so from now on. Where did the Mr. M. and the Ms. D. idea come from?" Diane asked.

"In the late 1960s and early 1970s, it became informal respect to use the Mr. or the Ms., along with the initial letter of the first name—thus, Mr. M., for me; Mr. D., for your father; and now, Ms. D., for you. This simplifies things for the students, and for us in what to call faculty," I said.

"Got it—back to the question about my father."

"Well, the fact of the matter is that your father was in a car with a student during spring break of 1975. The car was parked in a somewhat secluded area when police approached the car."

"And...?"

"The police reported to the superintendent of schools at the time, Mitchell Appletone, that an officer found a teacher and a student together in a parked car with no one else around."

"Do you know if anything other than talking was going on?" Diane asked.

"No. There was not. I am as sure as I can be that nothing else was going on. I was informed your father was trying to help a student get the assistance she needed. The student in the car at the time has also attested that your father was giving advice—and doing nothing else."

"Was the student's name revealed?" Diane asked.

"Yes, it has been. You could find out, but I will save you the trouble. The student's name then was Lydia Smith," I said.

"You said her name was Lydia Smith 'then.' What is it now? Why did she change it? Also, is she still living in Gorham?" Dianc asked.

"Yes, she is living here now. She changed her name after the incident because she wanted to start her life over again. There was some acrimony in Gorham about Mr. D., your father, being drummed out of town."

"Are you able to tell me what her name is now?"

"Yes, some of the teachers know. The former Lydia Smith is now April Danniels. She teaches with my wife Ana in the Gorham Central Elementary School."

"I would like to talk with April some time if she would be willing to tell me about my father."

"I will check with April through Ana to see if it is possible."

"Please do. Please do, Mr. M., I want to know as much about my father as I can learn."

"Diane, I can tell you this."

"Please do, Mr. M."

"Your dad was an outstanding and inspiring teacher."

"Yet, Mr. M., he lost his job."

"Yes. He did."

"So, Mark Blenchard, you are telling me that this 'outstanding' teacher, Derek Randallston—my father—lost his job for trying to help a student."

"Yes, I guess that is what I am saying."

"Mr. M., I hope you realize how difficult this is for me to understand."

Chapter 4: Helen

"April, do you know what happened to the woman you met when you were in New York City?" I asked. "I think her name is Helen."

"Her name is Helen, and no, Mr. M," April Danniels responded. "I have not heard from her or know anything about her whereabouts. However, I am thinking about going to New York over spring break and retracing the steps I took when I fled to the city over a decade ago."

"Why would you go back there? In retrospect, April, was it a good experience?" I asked.

"It wasn't necessarily a good experience. However, it had a major impact on my life."

"If you feel comfortable telling me, what was the impact?" I asked.

"I trust you, Mr. M., and feel comfortable explaining to you what happened," April said.

"I am glad you trust me, April. I am willing to hear as much as you wish to tell me."

"Well, Mr. M., I don't want to retrace all my steps while I was in New York City, and after all, that would take a while." April said. "As you may recall from my previous discussions with you about my trip, when I left Gorham, I spent time in the big city. I then went on to

Phoenix, Arizona and eventually made my way back to Gorham."

"I understand your reluctance to go over the details of your previous trip again. So, if you do go to New York during our break, how will you search for Helen?"

"I will go back to the hostel where I first met Helen. If I can find her, I will try to learn what has occurred in Helen's life since I last saw her."

After we talked, April prepared for her spring break. When the time came, April boarded a bus—the same mode of travel she took to New York when she first traveled there years ago.

April emailed me after she had been in New York for a couple of days: "Hi Mark. I hope all is well with you. I went back to the hostel where I first met Helen. A lot of time had passed, so I was not surprised to see there was an entirely new staff. No one there had ever heard of or about Helen."

I wrote back, "Thanks for your email about searching for Helen and not finding her at the hostel. What did you do then?"

"Well, Mark," April responded, "as you can imagine, I did not know where to turn, so I went to a social agency located close by. I asked a counselor and staff members in the agency where someone like Helen might end up. They said people in her situation often just disappear—never to be heard from again."

April continued, "So, Mark, apparently some people living precariously from day to day change their last names. I was told they do this because they may have criminal records, or just do not want to be found by anyone. This makes them virtually impossible to track. Sorry, Mark, I did not learn any more than that. I will be returning to Gorham in the next couple of days, and then we can talk more about anything else I learn."

I did not hear from April again until she returned from her trip. We met on the weekend for lunch. "I am assuming your effort to find Helen did not provide any more leads about what happened in her life. Am I right about that?" I asked.

"Yes, Mark, unfortunately I didn't discover any information about where Helen could be located or anything else about her." April responded.

"As teachers, is there anything we can teach our students that we learned from Helen's life and her disappearance?"

"Mark, I think there is some important educating we can do. We can derive a lot from Helen's life which might help in our teaching."

"What are you thinking of April?" I asked.

"As you already know from my New York experiences I have already told you about, Helen's trauma started with the guy her mother worked for who raped her mom and got away with it. My guess is there are a lot of guys who exploit women that way. Helen's mother had no recourse. As the child resulting from a rape, Helen had no resort either."

"April, as you have reported, when Helen was born her mother took care of her the best she could. That is the way I remember the story as you relayed it to me," I said.

"Yes, her mother took care of her the way she knew how. Helen was nine years old when her mother died. After her mother's death, Helen lacked a safe place to go. There was no one to take care of her as she grew to adulthood. She was on her own, surviving on the streets of New York."

"When you met her in the hostel, was she just surviving?" I asked.

"Yes. The youth hostel was the only home she knew

after her mother passed. I guess she was surviving—maybe not really living. Helen had a vulnerability about her."

"April, do you know anything else that would help us teach about these kinds of situations?"

"Sorry, Mr. M., other than what I have said I do not know much more. As I said, I have not heard from Helen or anything about her or people in similar circumstances since I left New York for Phoenix. Years have passed since then," April said.

"So, when you returned to New York during our spring break to try to locate Helen's whereabouts, there was no one in the hostel after the intervening years who had a clue as to how she could be found. Do I have that right?" I asked.

"Yes, that's right. There was no one I could find who was able to help. I have no idea what happened to Helen. This is life for some people—anonymity and off our radar."

"Unfortunately, I am afraid that is the case," I said.

"I feel strongly about this. How do we teach about the forgotten people who live lives of desperation, Mark? I mean circumstances like what Helen has had to face. There are a lot of people like her who experience similar misfortune and just disappear. They hit the streets—homeless and vulnerable—fending for themselves without resources," April said.

"What do you think the answer is to their situation, April, if there is one?" I asked.

"Mark, I lack answers; I wish I had some. But I believe we should learn more and then teach about the invisible people, because it is what is happening to lots of people who exist in the shadows. Imagine immigrants who are without documentation with no place to go. What happens to them?"

"I have no idea about that either. I believe we should find out," I said.

"Mark, you are the chair of our department, so you could call a meeting to discuss this. I want to explore these kinds of issues with our faculty and students."

"Thanks for the directive, April."

"Sorry, Mark, for being so bold to tell you what to do. I may be too brash doing so, but I am convinced we ought to teach about those who are destitute. These people have no home to go to. This results in a variety of societal ramifications."

"I understand your sense of urgency. You were in New York and I was not. You experienced things first-hand. So, absolutely—yes—we should teach about what it is like to be without any prospects of personal or public assistance. We should help our students understand the lives of these people," I said.

"We might get in trouble doing so. Teaching about the homeless is outside the purview of the prescribed curriculum, and, in a conservative place like Gorham, has little chance of being included in what we are instructed to teach," April said.

"Indeed, April, we just might get into difficulty with the school board and some members of the public," I said.

"Regardless, Mr. M., I believe it is the right thing to do. I am in for the long haul—teaching what really matters rather than always playing it safe. The conventional might allow us to keep a job but would shed the sacred honor our vocation requires. Without heart, a classroom is barren and lacks purpose. To cite Thomas Jefferson, 'A little rebellion now and then is a good thing.' So, Mark, are you with me?"

"Yes, April, I am all in with you, and I get the point about what Jefferson said. At some time in my life, I must stand for something. It is against every bone in my body to rebel. Teaching about the displaced and dispossessed, however, is a good place to start."

Chapter 5: Vote

"Hey, Mr. M., why should we bother to vote when we get old enough? It does not matter. Mr. M., it just doesn't do any good," Bettina, a student in my American government class, asked.

"Bettina, I need more explanation of what you are thinking when you say it 'doesn't do any good.' What are you saying won't do any good?"

"Voting won't do any good. I have been studying how our political system operates," Bettina said.

"What have you discovered?" I asked.

"Well, for example, look at the Electoral College. We are supposed to be electing a president for all the people—isn't that right, Mr. M.?"

"That is the theory. Go on, Bettina."

"Well, the person with fewer votes has won five times. The nineteenth century presidents who won without a plurality—John Quincy Adams, Rutherford B. Hayes, and Benjamin Harrison—were not successful presidents. And more recently, presidents George W. Bush and Donald Trump did not get the most popular votes."

"Well, Bettina and everyone, it will take some historical distance to judge if presidents Bush and

Trump will be deemed to have been good leaders of our country."

"Yah, Mr. M., we get that. However, based on the nineteenth century presidents who were not so good, why should we vote if the person with the most votes, and is supported by more of the electorate, loses. That makes no sense if we are, indeed, a democracy. Why, Mr. M., why does this happen?"

"You ask important questions, Bettina. However, isn't voting part of our responsibility as citizens?" I asked.

"Maybe, but if it does not make any difference to vote, then why do it? As we have learned since kindergarten, the person with the most votes should win. However, some presidential candidates have lost to the eventual president who received fewer votes. These minority presidents cannot rally the public behind them because the people did not choose them to lead the United States. I just don't get why we do it this way, and we are still doing it in the twenty-first century," Bettina said.

"Yah, Mr. M., I agree with Bettina. The president is supposed to represent us all. Therefore, the person who gets the most votes should be the president, but that doesn't always happen," Alice said.

"Alice, you indicated you agree with Bettina. Do you agree with everything she said?" I asked.

"Yes, I do—pretty much. My reasons are the same as Bettina's about how we elect presidents. Because of the Electoral College, we sometimes have a minority ruling over the majority. Mr. M., that is not a democracy. In a democratic country, the majority is supposed to rule, and each person should have only one vote. In our system for electing presidents, eligible voters in small states have more individual power when voting for president than those voters in large states," Alice said.

"Anyone else have a comment?" I asked.

"Yes, I do. I have been doing some research as Alice has. This is what I found, Mr. M.: For example, I read that because we use the Electoral College to elect presidents, each of Wyoming's 550,000 residents has the impact of 68 voters in California which has more than 34 million people in that state. There are many more states where one state's votes per person have more impact than another state. This is way out of whack for a country that calls itself democratic. Mr. M., you have to admit that," Andrew said.

"Mr. M., I am going to check out for myself the numbers Andrew just gave us regarding the relative power of one voter in Wyoming and California," Liz said.

"Don't you believe me, Liz?" Andrew asked.

"That isn't it, Andrew, but Mr. M. is always recommending we check things out for ourselves," Liz responded.

"Yes, Liz, Andrew, and everyone, doing your own research is a good idea," I said.

"Mr. M., I think what Andrew, Bettina, and Alice said is important. So, can you explain to us why we are called a democracy—which I have found is defined as the majority rules and each person has just one vote—when five times in United States history the person who was elected to represent the entire country had fewer votes than another candidate. In a democracy, the person receiving the most votes for president is supposed to win. Can you or anyone else defend why in the United States that does not happen?" Marvin asked.

"What do some of the rest of you think?" I asked.

"Mr. M., I believe that for an office like the president, the person representing all of us should be the person most voters in the United States have voted for. So, I agree with Marvin. If we are a democracy, why does the person receiving the most votes not win? Why is that the case, Mr. M.? WHY?" Mickey asked.

"I hear what you are saying, Mickey. The stance you, Bettina, Marvin, and Alice are taking illustrates one of the contradictions in our country when we call ourselves a democracy. Is that what you are saying?"

"Yes. Mr. M., that is what I believe we are saying," Mickey said.

"Why is that the case?" Bettina inquired. "We, as future citizens, want to know why."

"If what we have been saying is true and the United States governmental process is not a democracy, then what should it be called?" Richard asked.

"Right back to you, Richard. What do you think the United States government should be called?" I asked.

"Well, Mr. M., we pledge ourselves to a 'Republic for which it stands,' so maybe we should call ourselves a republic," Richard responded.

"Yah, Mr. M., as Richard said, we pledge to a republic. We don't pledge to a democracy," Shawn said.

"Does anyone else have anything to add to what Richard and Shawn just said?" I asked.

"Yes, Mr. M.," Adrian said. "The word democracy is not used in the *Constitution of the United States*. You are always telling us to check things out for ourselves, so last night I word searched the *Constitution*. I did not find the word democracy, but did find in Article four, Section four, this wording, in the *Constitution*: 'The United States shall guarantee to every state in this Union a Republican Form of Government....'"

"I agree with Adrian, Mr. M., democracy isn't even mentioned in the *Constitution*, but a 'Republican form of government' is," Madeleine said.

"Can anyone in class identify the differences between a democracy and a republic?" I asked.

"I would like to try, Mr. M."

"Go ahead, Vanessa."

"We are in fact a republic. I learned in my Latin class that if you break down a word from its Latin roots, then you can figure out what the word means," Vanessa said.

"So, where does 'republic' come from and what does it mean?" I asked.

"The English word 'republic' comes from Latin," Vanessa responded. "In Latin, republic means that the 'affair or matter goes back to the public.'"

"Oh, smarty-pants showing off with your Latin," Andrew interrupted.

"Andrew, please let Vanessa finish, then it is your turn," I said.

"Okay, Mr. M. I am sorry I interrupted Vanessa. Go ahead, Vanessa, with what you were going to say—sorry," Andrew said.

"Well, I believe the original Latin means that the matter goes back to the public for approval. A republic is nowhere near a direct democracy. A republic has representatives, but representatives can vote the way they want despite how their constituents may want them to do so. In a republic, those who contribute to campaigns have more influence on the elected representatives than regular voters who do not give any money. The average citizen doesn't vote sometimes because they believe the money-changers have stacked the deck," Vanessa said.

"Andrew—you want to respond again. What are your thoughts?"

"I am okay with the way Vanessa explained it. Campaign financing affects representatives. So, they might not vote the way their constituents want them to. They mostly vote the way their contributors want them to; money talks. I agree that those who contribute to political campaigns have more say than ordinary citizens. Mr. M., those who pay get to play," Andrew stated.

"Yah, wealthy people have more influence in who gets elected. Those who finance campaigns get more of what they want from the government," Patricia said.

"Some of the major people who influence campaigns own television stations and newspapers in local communities. Those sources are how people get information about candidates and the issues in their communities, state, country, and world—the folks who own things have power," Mitchel said.

"And, Mr. M., the owners of media outlets do not have to tell the newspapers and electronic media what to do—they know what to do to keep people tuned in and to sell newspapers. Most of the media is for profit so they give readers, viewers, and their owners what they want. If the media-types did not give consumers what they seek, the various media would not be in business because people wouldn't tune in to have their biases reinforced," Erica said.

"Mr. M., as Andrew and Erica said, 'money talks,' and I would say talks louder the more you have of it. It may not be 'quid pro quo' to use another Latin phrase, but campaign contributions have impact," Aaron said.

"What is quid pro quo? So, know-it-all, are you trying to one-up us?" Morris asked.

"No, Morris, I am not trying to be a nerd. I, like Vanessa, learned in Latin class what quid pro quo means. It is the idea that if I do something for you then you do something for me," Aaron responded. "Politicians and people in the news use the term all the time."

"Quid pro whatever sounds like a deal we would make in the streets," Jon said to laughter.

"I would like to get back to an issue Billy has raised in an earlier paper he wrote. He has done some research on whether the United States is a republic or a democracy. Billy, what did you find?" I asked.

"Mr. M., in addition to the Electoral College being undemocratic when electing presidents and having its roots in the slavocracy, there are other examples of practices in the government of the United States that are not democratic," Billy said.

"Okay, Billy, go ahead with other examples of governing problems in the United States in addition to how we elect presidents. Also, you used the term 'slavocracy.' What do you mean by that?" I asked.

"Well, if the enslaving states did not get their way in 1789, the *Constitution* would not have been ratified. So, the *Constitution* was tilted toward the states with the institution of slavery from the beginning. Ten of the first twelve presidents were slave-owners. They represented a nation that accepted slavery; thus, our country evolved out of a slavocracy. The system was stacked in favor of the status quo and conservatism from the beginning," Billy said.

"Are you sure, Billy? That 'slavocracy' comment sounds extreme to me," Katherine said.

"Yah, Katherine, I am sure. The *Constitution* was a compromise. The slave states would not have joined the union if slavery was eliminated in the United States at the time. And, yes, it is a fact that even presidents enslaved people, and some kept them enslaved throughout their presidencies and beyond," Billy responded.

"Billy, can you name the presidents who were slave owners?" Katherine challenged.

"Okay. I have notes on it," Billy said.

"Billy, if you can find your notes then go ahead and respond to Katherine about what you found," I said.

"Okay, Mr. M., I have my notes right here," Billy said.

"Who were the presidents who enslaved people?" I

asked.

"From my research, of the first twelve presidents, only John Adams and his son, John Quincy Adams, did not own enslaved people. The following presidents did enslave people—George Washington, Thomas Jefferson, James Madison, James Monroe, Andrew Jackson, Martin Van Buren, William Henry Harrison, John Tyler, James K. Polk, and Zackary Taylor." Billy recounted.

"And, hey, Mr. M., the enslavers made a lot of money off the enslaved peoples' labor," Micah said.

"I am going to do my own research. Not that I don't believe you, Billy, or what Micah just said, but I want to find out for myself," Katherine said.

"That is a good idea, Katherine, for all of us. It is important to hear what others have to say. However, it is essential to check information for ourselves. There is a lot of misinformation out there in the world, especially in the virtual world. So, make sure you use multiple sources and compare one with the other," I said.

"Yes. Mr. M., we are beginning to figure that out. You say that all the time," Kailae said to laughter.

"I guess I do but checking things out for yourselves through more than one source is important," I said.

"Got it, Mr. M. Got it," Tyrone confirmed, as other students chuckled.

"So, to go on, Billy. We have been discussing the Electoral College and whether it is democratic or not. So, do you—Billy—or anyone else have examples of other practices in United States' elections that are not democratic?" I asked.

"Sure, Mr. M. Many districts in the House of Representatives elections are gerrymandered which allows people in power to shape a district to improve the chances of their party winning. Such a practice is definitely not democratic," Billy said.

"Any other examples besides the Electoral College and gerrymandering districts? Brenda, you have your hand up."

"Yes, campaign money is another example," Brenda said. "It is way too influential in campaigns. We need public financing, because in our country's history a small percentage of people have wielded considerable power because they have the money and fund the campaigns. It is even more a factor today, because it costs so much to run a campaign with the high cost of television advertisements. All of this puts too much power in the hands of a few plutocrats."

"Brenda, please define plutocrat for us," I requested.

"Those who have the money rule, and plutocrats have the money," Brenda responded.

"Any other examples to add to Brenda's? Jason, you have a comment."

"Yes, Mr. M., as we have already discussed, the *Constitution* gives two senators to small states with less than a million people and just two senators for states with 20 to 30 times that many people. That is not a democracy — meaning one person, one vote — because one state can elect a senator with less than a million votes. Some other states need ten or twenty, or in the case of California, thirty times that many votes to elect a senator. That is nowhere near equal nor is it a democracy," Jason said.

"No, Jason, it isn't democratic, nor is it meant to be. The founders of the American government were against a direct democracy. The United States is a republic, the founders of this country wanted it that way, and that is the way it should be," Charona said. "As has already been mentioned, we pledge allegiance to a republic not a democracy."

"Charona, it sounds like you are against democracy," Peggy said.

"Yes, I am. The founders of our country feared an uneducated electorate, and I do too. And, in addition, the word democracy is nowhere to be found in the *Constitution of the United States*," Charona said.

"So, Charona, you said you are against democracy. Are you really?" Peggy challenged.

"Can I keep going and explain further?" Charona asked.

"Sure, Charona, go ahead," I said.

"If uninformed or mis-informed people elect our presidents, senators and representatives, our country would be in deep trouble," Charona said.

"We already are in trouble," Mitchel said as students laughed.

"Can I say something Mr. M.?"

"Sure, Jerome, go ahead."

"In our present way of doing things—I agree with Mitchel—we already elect some ignorant people who don't know what they are talking about. They have gotten us into trouble—some have put us into deep do-do," Jerome said to more laughter.

"Yah, Jerome, you seem to think it is funny. The founders of this country were smart enough to create a system so the people who are informed would control things. I believe we elect some good people in our system," Charona said.

"So, Charona, how did the founders of the republic create this system you like so much?" Jerome asked.

"Well, there are a variety of ways we are protected from the 'tyranny of the majority.' The Electoral College is one of the ways minority rights are protected. Small states having two senators is another. I agree with the founders of this country in keeping the majority, especially the uneducated, from controlling things."

"Why do you say that Charona?" I asked.

"I am in favor of keeping uninformed people from running our government. It is that simple. The smartest people should control things. I learned in another class that this guy, Plato, wrote in his book, *The Republic*, that the wisest people should make the laws," Charona said.

"Mr. M., in addition to what Charona just said, we discussed in the other course—the tyranny of the majority. We read part of Alexis de Tocqueville's *Democracy in America*. Tocqueville, a French writer, warned against the majority dominating the powerless when so-called democracy is let loose on the minority," Denisa said.

"Well, which is worse—tyranny of the majority or tyranny of the minority?" I asked.

"Both, actually, Mr. M. I believe minority rights need to be protected. That is why we have a Bill of Rights attached to our *Constitution*. We also have a system of 'checks and balances' in which the House of Representatives checks the Senate, the Congress checks the executive branch, and the judiciary makes sure the *Constitution* is followed. A good system I would say," Kieley said with a cryptic smile.

"Okay, the bell is going to ring in a few minutes," I said. "As we conclude class, I want to move us back to where we started this class to leave all of you with some questions to think about. Is Charona correct in what she says are the differences between a republic and a democracy? Also, if in a democracy uninformed people can rule, then where would that leave the United States if we did have more democracy? If Charona is right in what she is saying about a republic versus a democracy, then what are the implications for each of you as future citizens? Finally, will our system of checks and balances keep our governmental system in balance?"

"Beckie, you have your hand up. The class is going to end soon. So, what is it you would like to say?" I asked.

"Okay, Mr. M., I am for a democracy rather than a republic. I believe in one person, one vote, and the majority should rule. So, I disagree with what Charona has been saying," Beckie said.

"If we are going to have a democracy, we better make sure everyone has an equal chance to be educated before citizens get to the age when they can legally vote," Janet said. "Otherwise, people who don't know anything will be telling the rest of us what to do."

"Janet, on the other hand, if we already did have a democracy, we would have to make sure everyone is educated; the alternative would be chaos," Sarah said.

"Exactly, Sarah, but right now we aren't educating everyone for citizenship. I believe we should provide civic education for everyone before we have a full democracy," Janet responded.

"By the way, Mr. M., are we talking about a direct democracy or a representative democracy?" Rick asked.

"What is the difference, Rick?" I asked.

"A direct democracy would be citizens voting directly on issues. A representative democracy is when the qualified voters elect representatives who vote on issues representing the views of their constituents," Rick said.

"Which do we have Rick?" I asked.

"From the definition I gave, I would say we have a representative democracy which I believe could also be called a republic—requiring the consent of the governed—but it is not direct democracy."

"Okay, everyone, after hearing Rick's explanation I am going to leave our class with these additional questions to think about: Is the United States a democracy, a republic, or maybe something else? If we are going to have a democracy or a republic, and the people know little about history and civic government, then what will most likely happen? Also, do you agree with founding father James Madison who said, 'A popular government without popular information or the means of acquiring it, is but a prologue to a farce, or a tragedy, or perhaps both'?"

"That's a lot to think about, Mr. M. You ask a lot of questions and expect us to come up with the answers," Nathan said as the bell rang.

"Yes, Nathan, I do expect and hope you will do your own thinking, which is what we all have to do as citizens."

Chapter 6: Leaker

"Mark, there is a story I haven't told you." Lacey Walsh's comment at lunch during a professional meeting piqued my interest.

"I am listening. What's up?"

"I haven't told you the story because until recently I hadn't realized the importance of some of what happened in my previous job as a news anchor."

"Hmmm, Lacey, you have sparked my curiosity. Please go on," I urged.

"After talking with a friend who I first met at the television network where I worked, something is beginning to make sense to me now," Lacey said.

"I am still listening. This should be informative," I said with a pensive smile, not having any idea what I was about to hear.

"Okay, Mark, what I am going to tell you is another real-life media story that we both could use in teaching about the media. Although, we would have to use the information with care."

"I am always looking for good instructional material. So, what do you have?" I said.

"I believe what I have is important. One caveat, however, we can tell the story to our colleagues and the essence of it to our students, but we cannot identify people and places. If we did, someone could track the story to those involved. That could result in you and me having employment problems," Lacey cautioned.

"Geesus, Lacey, you have me attentive," I said. "And whatever you tell me, I will be careful what I say to others."

"Mark, we are going to have to be careful. This is big—it involves the presidency," Lacey said.

"The Presidency of the United States?!" I exclaimed. "Is that what you are talking about?"

"Yes, that is what I am talking about."

"Holy Toledo! Are you serious? You don't look like you are joking," I said.

"I realize that is about as strong as your language gets, but this is high-stakes. Yes, I am serious," Lacey said.

"I believe you are," I said as my voice dropped.

"I am going to use some circumlocution to convey what I have to say because my paranoia is way up. These people we are going to talk about can hurt you and me in variety of ways. Therefore, I am going to beat around the bush, but I think you will comprehend what I am talking about," Lacey said.

"You certainly have my full attention," I said.

"I don't even quite know what to make of what I am about to tell you. However, if I have figured out what may have been going on, then I do not like it. As we both know, Mark, the welfare of the country depends on obtaining accurate information."

"This is getting more interesting by the moment, and 'welfare of the country' claims are high-drama. I am assuming you are also serious about that comment," I said.

"Yes, Mark, I am serious. In fact, I could not be more

serious," Lacey said.

"As you stated, Lacey, getting accurate information is essential in self-government. I agree with you on that. So, my ears continue to be wide-open. You have created suspense, which must have been part of your job in the news business—getting people to stay tuned. Now you have me tuned in—go for it," I said.

"Okay, Mark, here goes. When I was talking recently with this friend who is still working at the network where I worked, I learned some things I had not thought possible for a news person to do."

"Are you able to identify anything about this person who provided you with the information?" I asked.

"No, I am not. In the case I am talking about—the person I talked to who furnished the information to me was and still is a real friend—not someone who will stab me in the back. In turn, I need to protect this person's identity."

"I understand. Go ahead Lacey," I urged.

"Alright, with all this build-up, I hope what I tell you is worth your time and interest, and by revealing it won't cause me and my friend problems. However, I wouldn't be telling you if I didn't think it is important," Lacey said.

"I will let you know if it is worth my time, and I don't think what you are about to say to me privately would cost your job, even though I don't know what information you have," I said.

"We will see about that—although, as you just said—you don't know what I am about to tell you," Lacey said with a nervous laugh.

"Ahh, I get it. Please go on," I said.

"Will do, Mark. So, here is the story: After I left the television business, my friend stayed with the company we had worked in together. At present, my friend is not telling anyone, but she is constantly searching for another job because of what she has observed at the television network. With all the machinations swirling around, she cannot stand working there any longer. However, she needs the paycheck and feels stuck there until she can find another way to make a living," Lacey said.

"This friend sounds central to your story. What did you learn from her?"

"Yes, she is essential to the story. She is the one who told me the vice president of the television network was a 'leaker.'"

"A what?" I asked.

"A leaker," Lacey said.

"What is that?"

"Well, Mark, a leaker provides information to others that is supposed to be closely held, confidential, and not traceable. In the case of this network vice president, she leaked to political operatives, to trusted friends, and to influential acquaintances in the news business."

"How did your friend know that the network's vice-president provided info that was confidential and closely held?"

"Let me say she just knew. She worked with senior management, overheard parts of phone calls, heard in-office conversations, and was frequently on the receiving end of written messages. Basically, as I indicated, she was positioned to learn things. She connected the dots. Her previous knowledge about politics and television news helped her figure things out even when the messages were masked."

"Did others know about the VP's behavior and what she was doing?" I asked.

"Others at the network may have gleaned slices of what was going on. However, my friend was closer to the action, had more pieces of various communications, and put two and two together. She was good at deciphering. Even if others at the network knew something, they just went along. In going along and getting along, they received steady—and for some of them—substantial paychecks," Lacey said.

"Please go on," I said.

"The VP proceeded to gather more and more power over network programming. As a result, she was able to spout her views to whomever would listen. However, she was careful and cute about how she communicated to her acolytes. She was also shrewd in what she conveyed to those sources who would distribute her messages through the media."

"How did she protect herself?"

"If anyone in the network had an inkling of what the VP was doing, my friend said no one dared talk about what the vice president was doing. No one said to my friend what they may have suspected—publicly at least. Fear all too often leads to silence. So, to this point, no one has outed her," Lacey recounted.

"But, Lacey, the media types like this VP are in the news business where truth and not misinformation should matter," I asserted.

"Yes, Mark, I realize that. However, her subordinates were afraid to talk about what they thought the VP might be doing. Apparently, anyone who revealed anything substantial found out the hard way that their time in the network was up. The VP used informants who employed hearsay about alleged indiscretions to control the voices who might reveal what they suspected. Besides, substantial income and the risk of losing it if one speaks out can have the effect of keeping those compensated with big bucks quiet. It by and large has worked."

"I am assuming the vice president leaking information is legal to do."

"I don't know, maybe as long as it isn't libelous it is protected speech," Lacey said.

"What do you see then as the major problem, Lacey, I mean as far as the news industry and leaking is concerned?" I asked.

"Well, it may not be illegal to leak, but the kind of leaking this person was doing is at the very least unethical for a news person. She is most likely still doing it," Lacey said.

"I am assuming what this VP is communicating is believable by those receiving the leaks," I said.

"Yes. I think others believe her and have believed her because in most cases she is confirming their biases," Lacey said.

"Therefore, she is communicating to others with similar points of view. Is that the case?" I asked.

"Yes, that summarizes it. In addition, though, I sensed she was also trying to convince those who needed convincing. And, because she is in the news industry and has access to information, she is considered a source. Good journalists would check out what she told them, but they listen first," Lacey said.

"Has she been effective, and does she continue to have influence in the leaking she is doing?" I asked.

"Yes. I believe she has been effective in propagating her point of view. And, because of her position in the news business, politicos and media types take her calls. She is essentially able to propagandize at will," Lacey said.

"At a news station, aren't you supposed to be neutral and not leaking information to one side or the other?" I asked.

"Yep. That is the presumed modus operandi.

However, even though news professionals try to look neutral and non-partisan, everyone has a point of view. We all believe we value truth and what we believe is right and is the truth. This VP believes her viewpoint is the right one, and that the other side is wrong. She apparently believes she is saving the American republic through her actions," Lacey said.

"But, Lacey, in the news business it is supposed to be just about the news, and reporters aren't supposed to take sides. 'You just report.' I realize I keep returning to this idea. Isn't that the principle?" I asked.

"Yes, Mark, you keep bringing this up. I mean, you are asking what a news person is expected and supposed to do as a reporter and not be in the business of furthering one side's point of view over another," Lacey said.

"That is what I am asking. I have assumed that a neutral search for the truth is codified in the profession's ethics," I said.

"Of course, Mark, the thesis is that people in the business of news are after the truth and that is the way the public believes it is supposed to be. In the case of this person, she thinks she is doing the right thing—the VP is a true believer. She believes she is being objective and is on the right side. Therefore, she is doing her job as she understands it. That is what makes it so frustrating and difficult to counter," Lacey said.

"I am still confused, so help me understand what happened. It sounds important. I want to make sure I get it," I said.

"Okay. Let me explain it this way—this vice president for programming was what many people would call to the right of the political center—a political conservative. Although she would say she is right down the middle—or as she would claim—'I am neutral.' She confounds being conservative with being neutral. She is positive her alleged neutrality is the right way to view things—even though it is to the right on the political spectrum—if you can follow that," Lacey said.

"I think I can," I said. "It sounds, Lacey, as if like other true believers, this person you are talking about deems she is the pure one."

"Yes, Mark, and she believes the other side is wrong and even villainous."

"Please explain that to me."

"The VP has convinced herself that she is untainted, and that liberals are harmful to the country," Lacey said.

"Okay, I get that. How does she convey, or as you say it—leak—her beliefs to others?" I asked.

"Well, this VP learns something political while working in the network, and then plants it in the hands of her allies in the political world—conservatives. In her mind, conservatives are the good people. These 'good people' use the negative information about liberals and place it in the media—preferably in a medium that does the most harm to liberals."

"Specifically, how does she pass along what she thinks she knows?" I asked.

"She conveys it to political operatives through phone calls or sends it by secure electronic messaging. Her objective is to get the negative hearsay about liberals into the 'right' hands, so it gets out to the public and hurts the liberal cause."

"Who did she think are the liberals, and how has she defined them?"

"She defined liberals as anyone to the left of her. Liberals are those other than a right winger like herself and her friends in politics," Lacey said.

"How does she prevent getting outed?" I asked.

"She is coy. If someone or more than one guest is in

the television studio's waiting room before an interview, she engages them in 'off-the-record' discussions. For her though—it is never off' the record. She feeds what she learns from the guest to her political buddies. The VP and her confidants are in unwritten and unspoken deals with each other. They protect each other as sources. She provides what she believes she knows to her 'anonymous' associates who find ways to get the message in the various media.

"Therefore, they all win—the leaker gets the message out, the recipient gathers the scoop, and the news outlet gets credit for revealing the story whether true, false, or incomplete."

"Holy mackerel. Lacey, this astounds me. What I get from what you are saying is this leaker ran a network operation that appeared fair in presenting a variety of views through the screen. Off air, she was and is a propagandist. Is that what you are saying?" I asked.

"Yes, that was what she was doing while I was at the network, and she is still leaking."

"How do you know she is still leaking?"

"A glass of wine and a friend from the network brought me up to date," Lacey said.

"Am I correct that no one discovered what was going on and outed this person? Do I have that right?" I asked.

"You do. No one I know of unearthed what was going on. None of these so-called smart people at the network figured it out enough to communicate to those outside the organization that there was a gross manipulation of information right under their noses. Moreover, if anyone knew anything about what the VP did in passing on negative information about liberals to those outside the organization—and this VP found out about this person—she would blackball forever anyone who outed her, or even tried," Lacey said.

"She sounds like she could hurt someone badly in the industry and is powerful enough to do so," I said.

"Yes, Mark, that is correct. Also, the vice president was careful in covering her tracks. You could scour the Internet and not find the word 'leak' anywhere near her name. As I mentioned, she was careful. Communiques were in-person conversations and phone calls—coded when necessary."

"Surreptitious messaging."

"Yes, Mark. In the sense that if someone overheard a phone call, they would not be able to decode what was actually being communicated," Lacey said.

"Can you give me an example of how this coding worked?" I asked.

"Yes, for example, the VP might say, 'Arthur was with Bill last night at the theatre.'"

"What does that message mean when it is decoded?" I asked.

"Because the person receiving the message knew the code, it would translate into 'Ashley was with Bill last night in his hotel room.'"

"Why is that problematic? They could have been having a business meeting."

"Well, both Arthur and Bill are married to someone else. Arthur is the pseudonym for Ashley that only the VP and the other person on the line know. It is left to the imagination what kind of business they were conducting in that hotel room."

"That is still not proof of anything."

"No, unless the sender and the receiver knew what the coded message means," Lacey said.

"What did it mean?" I asked.

"They were having sex. Mark, you continue to be way too innocent. They were screwing," Lacey said.

"Ahh. I see." I said.

"Actually, Mark, there are even more skillful machinations than that—I think you get the basics of the intrigue," Lacey said.

"I am afraid I do. You mentioned 'more skillful machinations,' and did the VP ever enrich herself in this process?" I asked.

"I will respond to the enrichment question. In short, she was careful."

"So, there is no money trail."

"I didn't say that," Lacey responded.

"Did she profit through sharing information?" I asked.

"As I said, she was careful."

"This is really getting interesting. Back to my question—was she financially rewarded?"

"Well, she sold her house and an additional property for good prices."

"Meaning?"

"A political financier who worked under the radar—with an agenda to promote in line with her politics—gave her the high price she was asking for her home. A company this guy controlled bought her other property also for way more than it was worth."

"What?" I exclaimed. "This sounds bizarre—almost conspiratorial."

"The VP asked considerably more than what houses in the neighborhood were going for, and she got it. I believe she knew she would get it. Her neighbors benefitted as well, because her real estate sale increased the value of their homes when it came time for them to sell. You know, the 'comparable price' thing. So, there was more than one winner in the transactions. Although, you might argue the American people were the losers because of the misinformation she had conveyed and would continue to convey."

"How would she have known she could do this? I

mean get the high price for her property."

"The prospective buyer may have communicated what she could get for selling. I do not know for sure, but that may have been what happened. I am merely speculating about how all this went down. What I do know is that the VP is well-heeled today," Lacey said.

"So, she could have known she would get the high price and make out really well. Is that what you are saying, Lacey?"

"Yes, Mark. When I saw her in the office after the sale, it was clear she was happy with the high prices on both her properties. And, as I said, I believe neighbors were delighted too because those who were on their way to retirement in warmer climes could get a higher price because of what a comparative home sold for. So, my guess is no one said anything because they all made out well in selling their property on their way south or to some tropical island. There are no complaints when everyone makes out like bandits."

"Cute. Really cute. So, Lacey, this VP made money without leaving a money trail," I said.

"Yup, Mark. Those of us who were in the news industry knew there were ways to do well—so to speak—and not get caught. However, very few professionals would do what this VP did in this case or do anything like it. However, I believe that is how it went down."

"Geesus."

"And, Mark, there is more," Lacey said. "The person who bought the house has never lived in it."

"Who has?" I asked.

"Well, the house has been used to store stuff. Also, when this new owner's friends and colleagues come to the area, they stay in the house rent free unless they have an expense account then the occupant pays top dollar to the landlord," Lacey said.

"Did anyone secretly record the VP when she was leaking information which resulted in her gaining financial largess?"

"Well, Mark, even if they did hear what was being said, as I mentioned earlier—the VP spoke primarily in code—words and symbols only the recipient understands. You know, Mark, you and Ana must have conversations using shorthand that only you and your significant other understand. Of course, the meaning of what is said between some married couples would be denied if anyone got close to deciphering, especially if any rumormongering was potentially slanderous—same with the VP and her messaging—deny, deny, and then deny some more."

"How then could you understand what was going on when this person was speaking in code if you weren't in on it?" I asked.

"Because from my desk close by, I kept hearing the conversations. It is possible to glean the message if you hear enough of it and pay attention to the repetitions. The interchanges had a rhythm to them. I heard a lot of conversations and figured it out. I knew her well enough, so I could interpret what others occasionally overhearing her could not."

"Did she succeed in what she intended to do?"

"She did. Because of her actions, there were some unfortunate outcomes for some people."

"What were those 'unfortunate outcomes'?" I asked.

"The VP made phone calls and dropped negative information about people she suspected might be in a position to out her or cross her in any way. As the result of the VP's phone calls and her information leaks, good people lost their jobs and reputations. Also, several people were ruined financially."

"That seems extreme and bizarre. How did that

happen?"

"When she or her minions accused suspects of infractions—real, imagined, or completely made-up—the accused had to defend themselves and fight for their jobs. It cost them a bundle, especially when it involved questions of illegality. Some of the accused spent whatever resources they had to defend themselves. This resulted in bankruptcy for some, and to add to the indignity—they lost jobs and were ousted from the industry because the word got out about the alleged indiscretions—plus, the amorphous, 'they are not loyal' allegations," Lacey said.

"What happened to those who were forced out? I asked.

"Some found another profession, and to my knowledge, never worked in politics or journalism again."

"This doesn't sound fair, Lacey. And, you said this woman has gotten away with it."

"Yes. She has. And, Mark, here is the kicker."

"What's that?"

"She got a promotion and received a bonus and a higher salary. The people she critiqued could not fight for their jobs or even defend themselves. She kept her leaks anonymous. Some of those she went after did not have the money to hire a lawyer. In the interim, the VP collected performance awards and scooped financial rewards."

"Geesus. Why are you telling me this, Lacey?"

"Because, Mark, I think we ought to teach about it. We should avoid naming names and to do so could get us into a heap of trouble, but we should help our students understand how the so-called 'real world' works. It is rough out there, and the stakes are high."

"We have a job to do. Getting only one side of the story in the news warps our attempts to develop informed citizenship," I said.

"Yes, it does. And, Mark, this VP is well-connected and growing even more powerful. If I were still in the industry and I said what I just said to you, and it got to the VP that I have been talking, I would be toast. I would have difficulty ever finding a job in the industry again—maybe never. She and her allies could hurt me attempting to find any job, even going back to my job waiting on tables—especially if the powerbrokers know the restaurant's owner or could find someone who does," Lacey said.

"The VP sounds like a dangerous person to provoke."

"Yes, she is, Mark. The VP has power and has cover from the top of the organization. She has protected the Chief Executive Officer, and he protects her. They are close friends—real close friends—if you get what I mean," Lacey said.

"Ahh, this time I believe I do."

"I am glad," Lacey said grinning.

"Why didn't she just run for office to bring about change consistent with her views, and do it that way?" I asked.

"It is quicker the way she and others who are in control do it. They don't bother with the slower political process," Lacey said.

"Lacey, I want to go back to that question. Even though the VP had an ideology—a conservative one—she never ran for political office and probably never will. Is that what you are contending?" I asked.

"Yes, that is what I am saying. She would have had to raise lots of money to run for office. Besides, for her cause, running a network gives her cover. Being in the news business has enabled her to appear neutral. Thus, as a powerbroker she has been able to push her ideology and causes behind the television screen's ersatz objectivity."

"Should we teach about what you have learned through your work in television?" I asked.

"Yes, Mark, it may be risky—but yes—we should teach about what we know. Even though it might mean the end of my career, I am not backing down, sitting down, or standing down," Lacey said.

"It will take some courage to teach truth to power," I said.

"Yes, it will take some courage. I have already told you the VP boosted conservative causes. In addition to those efforts, she leaked information gained at the network to those who supported conservative candidates' campaigns, including promoting candidates for the presidency of the United States from 1968 through 2016."

"Oh my—this is big. A person in the news business shouldn't be pushing any candidate's election," I exclaimed. "Is there anything else?"

"Yes, there is. During her long career occupying various positions in the television network, she tried to divide liberal groups by leaking to one faction of Democrats or the other. She knew what she was doing and was and is a master political manipulator," Lacey explained. "She thought she was the righteous one. As a result of convincing herself of her purity, she did what she thought she had to do to save the country. She reckoned the candidates she supported had been undercut by the bad guys—the liberals," Lacey said.

"You see, Mark, this network vice president was convinced that liberals had sandbagged conservatives running for the presidency of the United States. When the conservatives did get elected, like Richard Nixon and Ronald Reagan, then the canard she and her political devotees promoted is that the liberals lied about these two Republican presidents. Then, she believed, the liberals in the media would under-cut conservative administrations through slanting the news. As a result, conservative candidates' programs could not get through the legislative process."

"Lacey, this is important history. How are you sure what you are telling me is factual?" I asked.

"I have had to figure it out—two and two equals four not five as in the novel, *1984*. The VP did not tell anyone at the network what she really thought about history or politics except for dates and places. She was pretty coy in refraining from revealing her ideology," Lacey said. "She is what Eric Hoffer defined as a 'true believer.' She is certain she knows what is best for the United States. She has no doubt that liberals sabotage what is best for the country and are not acting in America's best interests. She employs the network as a front and as a cover to further her political advocacy."

"So, Mark, even though she has worked her way up in the network over the many years in the only organization she has ever been gainfully employed—moving from answering phones to an executive office–her colleagues appear to have no clue about her activity, and still do not. Balance is the network's mantra, but behind the scenes the VP is anything but balanced."

"Lacey, I am stunned. This person uses her position at the network to further her political agenda," I said.

"Yes, she has in the past, does so now, and I am convinced will in the future. She may not have set out to do it, but she has become a consummate propagator. She works the phones all day long. Nothing was or is put in writing. Any notes she keeps are cryptic. For the ruse to work, it must be kept close, with few people even sniffing what she is up to. As I have said, those who even smell her leaks find trouble if they reveal what they discover. She just despoils the political ethos though employing the network's alleged impartiality as a shield to further her political passions. It has worked for years."

"How do we teach this in our classes?" I asked.

"With great care. These people have power—she has power. So, teach about it with care and deliberation—but teach about it we must."

"Lacey, did you ever say anything about this publicly or to anyone?"

"No, I have not—until now, and just to you, Mark," Lacey said. "In explaining it to you I finally realize the full importance of what I have been telling you."

"So, Lacey, now what?"

"Teach without fear, Mr. M. That is what we must do—teach without fear."

Chapter 7: Jail

"Mr. M., I swear to God, I didn't do it," Ernie Blake said when I visited him in the County Jail.

"Ernie, I appreciate what you say may be true. However, I need to know the whole truth to help you."

"Okay, Mr. M. I will tell you as much as I can. I was there during the break in, but I didn't break the windows and I didn't steal the money or nothing," Ernie said.

"The fact you were there could make you culpable even though you did not participate in the actual robbery. So, who did rob the store?"

"I can't tell you that," Ernie said.

"Why not?" I asked.

"If I do, they will kill me."

"What!" I exclaimed.

"Mr. M., I am afraid. They said they would kill me. That's what they said they would do."

"Ernie, hold on, what did you say they are going to do to you? And who are they?"

"They do what they say they are going to do," Ernie said. "As gang members, they have taken a vow to do what they are ordered to do for the benefit of the gang. They do what the group is instructed to do, or else."

"Ernie, you said 'or else.' What do you mean by that?"

"The 'or else' vow is drummed into those of us in the group. If we disobey the gang's leaders, then they will eliminate you forever. And I mean forever."

"Do you really mean forever?" I asked.

"Yah, Mr. M., FOREVER. There is no escape from the gang and there is no sense trying—they find who they are looking for. There is no getting away from them even in jail and prison.

"In jail and in prison, you are a sitting duck. They WILL find you if they are after you. I am between a rock and a hard place. Mr. M., I need help, but nobody can help me. I got into something way over my head. Oh, Geesus," Ernie said as his voice broke.

"Ernie, are you sure about this? Because if you are, then these people in the gang are dangerous and you may be in trouble."

"Yah, Mr. M., that's what I have been trying to tell you. I am in trouble and these guys will be after my ass if they know I am talking to you," Ernie said.

"Tell me more," I said.

"M. M., I can't tell you no more—I told you that. The gang is powerful. If I talk and turn any of them in, I will be eliminated. What would be left of me would be put in a meat grinder. Nobody can protect me. They will not leave a trace."

"There is no getting away, no matter what you do. Is that what you are saying?"

"Yes. They will chase after me no matter where I go. They will do away with me. They won't leave nothin' left to bury."

"To understate your dilemma, Ernie, this does not sound good."

"It isn't. Mr. M. As I said, I got in way over my head. If I say anything about them, they are going to shut me up for good and probably will anyway if anyone sees me talking to anyone, especially with you—there won't be no evidence of what happened to me. They are good at covering things up."

"Are you sure, Ernie, about all of what you are saying?"

"Yah, they done it to other people. They have spies everywhere and will know if anyone betrays them."

"Have they told you specifically they would get you?"

"They don't have to. I know what they do to snitches, and it ain't pretty—I would be toast and that is no exaggeration."

"Ernie, you keep saying 'they,' and haven't told me yet. Who are THEY?

"Mr. M., you have to believe me that I did not steal nothing. I can't tell you who they are and who did what."

"Why not tell me? I will keep it to myself. You can trust me," I said.

"The gang members are sworn to secrecy, and if anyone in the gang breaks the vow—the vow-breaker is done for. And for traitors, things happen to their families. If they even see me talking with you...well.... Mr. M., I need you to get the hell out of here because I might be seen with you."

"Ernie, you mentioned your family. What is it—I mean—what happens to families?"

"They will go after my family," Ernie said, his voice trembling.

"By 'go after,' what do you mean?"

"They will beat up or even kill some of my family members—one by one. To make sure everyone gets the message, they will mutilate as many of my family members as they think is necessary to get their point across and scare the shit out of squealers—like me. And, as you can see, Mr. M., it is working on me."

"Do they usually get away with terrorizing people?"

I asked.

"Yah, Mr. M., they do. At least, they do most of the time."

"Oh, my God, Ernie. If this is all true, oh my God," I said not knowing what else to say.

"Mr. M., this gang is not fooling around."

"Ernie, to understate again, I see the problem. They have frightened you—panic is killing you right now."

"You may be right, Mr. M., but I ain't talking. I will not say no more. I wish you to go now, Mr. M."

"Ernie, I can't help you and no one else can help you if I and the authorities don't know who is threatening you and your family."

"I told you. I was there during the break-in, Mr. M. You must believe me that I was there and will not say no more about what happened. It is best for you to leave me alone," Ernie pleaded.

"I do believe you, but that doesn't help you or me much if I don't know what is happening," I said.

"As I keep telling you, Mr. M., I can't tell you no more."

"I can call a lawyer for you."

"I won't talk to no lawyer," Ernie said.

"How about the police? Will you talk to them?" I asked.

"No. No—not the police. God, Mr. M., are you trying to get me killed?"

"If you won't talk to a lawyer or the police, then law enforcement can't help you."

"Mr. M., I realize that—geesus, I am walking dead right now. Please, Mr. M., leave me alone. I have enough problems without being seen talking with you," Ernie said.

Ernie and I kept circling—talking around each other for a few more minutes. Ernie was not budging from his stated position, "I can't tell you," and, "please, Mr. M., leave me alone."

Shortly after meeting with Ernie, I received an anonymous call from someone asking me to go back to see Ernie in jail. The caller said, "It is important, and don't call the police station—just go."

I rushed to the jail. An agitated and frightened Ernie told me, "Mr. M., there have been threats made on my family. I told you that would happen. They know the addresses of my family members—where they live, where they work, where they go to school. What should I do?"

"I suggest we tell the police and alert them to the threats," I said.

"Are you sure that is a good idea?" Ernie responded.

"We have to do something, and that is the best option I can think of. So, yes, Ernie, I believe we should alert the police," I said.

"Yah, I guess we should. It may be the only hope. But what, Mr. M., should we do besides tell the police to protect myself and my family?"

"I don't know, Ernie, I am going to have to think about it. I will have to get back to you."

"I don't know what to do either. I am so upset. I just don't know what to do."

"Ernie, I am going to report to the police officers what you have said about the threats to your family. The police may have some ideas on how to protect you and your family."

"I guess you have to do that," Ernie agreed reluctantly.

"Yes, I believe I do," I said.

"Oh my God, Mr. M., they will get me in here. They will get my family. They will find out where I am. I am trapped in jail. I am a sitting duck, and my family is out there without protection."

After leaving Ernie, I felt helpless as a teacher and as a person. Ernie, frantic and afraid, did not have many alternatives—neither did I. Ernie's reluctance to report the threats made against him and his family to the authorities left me with few options. At the end of our meeting in his jail cell, he realized I would have to inform the police about the threats. It was the only alternative he had.

I returned home after meeting with Ernie. After thinking about what to do, I realized I had to go directly to the police and tell them everything I knew.

As soon as I could reach the police department by telephone, I arranged to meet with them in person at their headquarters. Upon arrival at the station, I stated to the commanding officer everything I understood about Ernie's predicament.

I went to Bailey High after going to the police station. I spent the rest of the evening completing school-related tasks.

The next morning, I called the jail to check on Ernie. A police officer answered the phone. After she verified who I was, she said, "I am sorry, but we found your student, Ernie Blake, dead two hours ago."

"Oh no!" I cried. "How did he die?"

"We don't know yet, Mr. Blenchard. I will have someone notify you once it has been determined how the young man died."

Chapter 8: Emails

"We will be meeting in front of the Town Hall. As you know, Jake, because of the school employment rules regarding political activity we must assemble after school hours. I will be there around quarter past four tomorrow afternoon. Can the two of us meet briefly before school begins?" I wrote in an email to Jake Spanner.

"Yes. I will meet you at the Main Street Coffee Shoppe at 6, and as planned I will be there at the Town Hall after school tomorrow," Jake responded.

Jake and I met for coffee as arranged. After we talked about the planned assembly at the Capitol, I asked, "Okay, Jake, but before you go, I have a question for you. I believe the emails we have received recently, including the last one announcing our meeting place, are through the school system's server. Is that correct?"

"Yes, Mark, that's right. What are you thinking? Is there a problem with that?" Jake asked.

"Possibly. Sending emails through school property, even without using the school system's email address, is enough for the town council to claim we are using government property for political purposes," I said.

"Do you believe they would actually pursue that

avenue? The demonstration is planned for after school—not on school time. So, what is the problem?" Jake asked. "In fact, Mark, I doubt there will be any difficulty."

"Maybe—maybe not. The school administration could contend we are using school-owned computers to send messages from the school's system making it look like it is an official message conducting school system business. This would be especially problematic if we use our school email address, which is prohibited for anything that is not authorized by school administrators," I asserted. "Teachers organizing an action against the school system is obviously not something the school board endorses."

"Alright, Mark, I can see where you are going with this. Is that why we generally meet before school and in town rather than on school property," Jake said.

"Yes. Discussing an action against the school system should be done off school property," I said.

"Ahh, I am getting it," Jake said.

"I am glad you are. The prohibition against using school property for political or personal purposes is especially problematic if we are conducting union business against the administration. The powers that be would then have something to use against us. They would have a solid legal basis for doing so."

"This seems minor to me," Jake said.

"It may seem minor to you, but It isn't minor to those in control. Especially, if the messages sent are for preparing a possible strike against the school system. The administration could contend we are using school property to organize against the district's best interest. If that is their argument, they might be right," I said.

"What if I send the message on a school computer from my personal email address? That must be okay."

"Jake, if you use school property—meaning using

a school-owned computer—then you could still have a problem."

"Okay, I see the logic. However, what if I send the message after school hours?" Jake asked.

"Jake, you are pushing the envelope to the point of being ridiculous. As I suggested, if you use school property for personal purposes or for messages other than those officially sanctioned—on or through any school property at any time—it is a problem."

"What you are saying to me sounds trivial and not worth our time worrying about. Are you sure about this, Mark?" Jake asked.

"No, I am not absolutely sure it would get us in trouble. However, if we are using school property to further a political issue, then it seems to me the administration would have to answer the question of whether we broke the rules or not. In any event, it could be against the usage rules. So, to make a long story short, I wouldn't recommend taking a chance by using school property—the school board has the fiduciary power concerning the use of school facilities and school time," I said.

"How then do we organize in order to defend our rights and communicate our positions?" Jake asked.

"We have to do it off school property, with our own equipment, on our own time, and using our own dime," I answered.

"It seems as if the people in control have all kinds of ways to stay in control, and they can curtail our capacity to affect change."

"Ditto that," I said.

"Mark, I need to go back to where I started. This use of the school's email system really does seem to be a petty infraction to me."

"It probably is minor, but potentially against school board policy and they have the legal authority. So, any infraction—even a seemingly trivial one—can be made into a big deal and can be blown way out of proportion. We might not see it that way, but those in control could and I believe would. They have the power to enforce their position."

"How about if someone uses the school's email to wish a sister happy birthday?"

"Jake, I realize you keep bumping the issue to its extreme. If no one complains or checks, then...maybe then it passes by. However, technically it seems to me wishing your sister happy birthday is personal. To use a school computer to do so is not a big taboo, but why challenge the authorities and give them any reason to go after you or our teachers' union?"

"Okay, okay, Mark. You have convinced me, at least partially. Some of this seems absurd even though I can see what you are saying has a certain logic to it."

"It may seem absurd, but we are the employees, and they are the employer. They make the rules. Our choice is to obey the rules or vamoose," I said.

"So, from this discussion, I get it that we need to be careful what we do on school property and how we use it. The facilities used for professional purposes, by and large, is alright. However, government property used for personal reasons—not so much. I think I have it. Do I?" Jake asked.

"Yes, and political actions are especially verboten, particularly when they are against the school system which funds the means of communication. When it comes to anything that looks like political activity—and a union action is political—using public property is a bad idea. School administrators can access anything we write on school owned property. So, better not write your boyfriend or girlfriend either."

"I get it. However, I am going to push back once more:

What if a teacher is writing an email from their school account to inform a spouse or partner that you have an event after school and will be late for dinner. Is that problematic?" Jake asked.

"Again, Jake, you are—shall I say—shoving it. You probably won't get in trouble for telling someone you will be 'late for dinner,' but theoretically—you know the drill by now," I said.

"I am afraid I do. It is the school system's property and if they want to get you on something—like using school property for anything personal—and you have used the school computer for something remotely 'personal' you have given them something to use against you if they want to."

"Yep, Jake, you've got it."

"Do you have any actual examples of administrators going after a teacher for minute infractions?" Jake asked.

"Yes, I do. Mitchell Appletone, a former superintendent of schools in Gorham, was infamous for getting rid of people he wanted to through citing transgressions. Even though they were admittedly minor, to Superintendent Appletone they were nevertheless infractions that should be punished if he had a hankering to do so. Derek Randallston was one of the teachers Appletone removed from the school system for an indiscretion that may not have been one at all. Appletone ousted him, sent him packing. Do you remember what happened to him?"

"Yes. I do. It is a cautionary tale well known by educators in this school system—Appletone won, Derek lost, and Gorham's students were deprived of a good teacher," Jake said.

"Ex-superintendent Appletone had a whole list of petty violations he collected and could use against people he did not like, or people who did things he did not approve of. He specifically punished employees who violated his unwritten, but furtively communicated dictums. He seemed to enjoy dishing out the punishments. There are school board members right now in Gorham who will remove any teacher if we give them a reason to do away with any of us who are perceived as trouble-makers," I said.

"So, it is best that we don't give them something to use against us. Is that what you are saying?" Jake asked.

"Yes, that would be prudent," I responded.

"How do we get organized then and fight for our rights if we can't communicate with each other?" Jake asked.

"Good question. I would recommend doing it carefully by keeping our organizing off school property and out of school time," I responded.

"If we have to do all this planning off school property and on our own time then that encroaches on our family time and getting prepared for class," Jake said.

"That's correct. The school board pays administrators to watch for any misuse of public property and time. We must use personal time to fight for our rights and get what we need for our students. And, as you said, this may affect time with family. The administration may not particularly care about our personal needs and wants. Jake, I realize you do care. However, the bottom line is if we are to organize it has to be using our respective resources," I said.

"That doesn't seem fair. The administrators are being paid to keep us in line. We are not paid when questioning their power. They are holding and able to deal the cards in a loaded deck," Jake said.

"Well, that is the way it is. They have the state-mandated authority," I stated.

"It still doesn't seem fair. Where does that leave us

Mark?" Jake asked.

"Well, Jake, you are right. It seems unfair—there are many things in life that are not fair. We are not in a strong position when it comes to organizing and fighting for our rights and promoting a quality education for our students. Indeed, the controllers of the system are in control."

"Do we have any options? Jake asked.

"One big one we have never used in Gorham," I responded.

"And, Mark, what is that?"

"To withdraw our labor and negotiate better conditions to educate our students."

"Are you saying what I think you are?" Jake asked.

"Yes," I said.

"The big option then is to...I don't want to say the word until you do," Jake said.

"Okay, Jake, I get the hesitancy on your part. But if we cannot obtain what we need to educate our students, the option we have left is to—well, let me spell it out for you—S-T-R-I-K-E."

"Ouch! Yes, Mark, that is the big step to take."

"Correct again, Jake! We need to realize that to strike against our employers for what we believe is right is a major action that can risk our well-being and future in our chosen profession," I said.

"I realize, Mark, it has taken a long time for me to get the point. However, I get it now—I get it," Jake said. "We may have to withdraw our labor and that is a very serious step to take."

"Yes, it is, Jake. Yes, it is," I said.

"Geesus," Jake exclaimed. "Geesus!"

Chapter 9: Strike?

"Ana, it is against every bone in my body to walk out of my classroom. It will mean leaving my students without their teacher. As you know, Honey, teaching is sacrosanct to me. I will only vacate my desk if I think to do so would be for the greater good of my students," I said.

"I know that, Mark. I will support whatever you decide to do," Ana assured me.

"Ana, as faculty, we have been pushed and pulled by those who control the school system. Some board members and town council members keep education budgets down to campaign for election to a higher office as fiscal conservatives. In the meantime, many of our students receive less of an education than they are entitled. Our students deserve more. I believe we adults must act. I and my colleagues do not want to continue working under the present conditions. We want the opportunity for a better education for our students."

"I understand what you are saying, Mark. I realize you must do what you believe is best for your students. Whatever you decide to do, we will be fine," Ana said.

"I hope so, Honey. I hope so."

"Mark, we will be alright. I am sure we will."

"I appreciate the support, Ana. I had previously

explained to Jake Spanner that going out on strike is the big step. It means removing our labor, and in some places breaking the laws prohibiting public employees from striking."

"Is Gorham one of those places where it could be against the law?" Ana asked.

"I don't know for sure if our action will violate any laws, but I believe teachers going on strike is a violation. I will have to check on the legality of what we might do."

To discuss our options, Ana and I invited our potluck dinner group to our home.

Bailey High social studies teachers Angela Tremonte, John Browne, Charles Yates, Jake Spanner, and Zack Barber attended as did media literacy and social studies teacher, Lacey Walsh. Also attending were high school English teacher, Cheryl Wattsen, art teacher Karla Betts, and Gorham Elementary School teacher, April Danniels. Ana and I hosted the potluck.

After we settled with drinks and food, I asked the potluck group, "What should we do? We are constantly pushed around in our efforts to educate our students. The administration is picking us off one by one for alleged indiscretions. If not the 'unauthorized use of email,' it will be another allegation. So, what to do?"

Angela Tremonte responded, "We need to hit the streets. If Claudia Pace were here, she would agree with me. We need to act. Our students' educations depend on it."

"Angela, I am sorry, but you sound like Megan Straffa when she was here. I, too, am against what is happening. However, striking is not an action I am ready to take, and there are significant questions about the actions and if they are legal. In fact, I do not believe it is legal for public employees to strike in this state," Charles Yates said.

"I don't usually agree with Charles, but I can't afford to miss a paycheck. So, even though I am sympathetic to the cause, I am not prepared to support a strike even if it were legal. Those in control have all the cards in their favor. They make the rules and the laws," Jake Spanner said.

"I thought you were what we call a 'liberal,' Jake. I guess not when it comes to taking an action that might actually make a difference," John Browne said.

"I have a family—you don't, John," Jake said.

"The fact you have a family is the very reason why you should be fighting for a better education for everyone. Teachers should be compensated fairly, and we need basic supplies with which to teach for our students to learn," John responded.

"Of course, John, I am for a better education for everyone, including my children, but the risks of losing a steady paycheck or even losing my job is a cost I can't pay," Jake said.

"Hooray for Jake. You are supposed to be a liberal. Welcome to the conservative club. I am glad you have seen the light," Charles said.

"Not exactly, Charles, I am still on the liberal side. A 'sick-out' would be safer than just walking off our jobs. It has been used successfully around the country. We just call in sick—that is all. We use our sick days which is something we all have," Jake said.

"I am not sure that will work, Jake. What do we do when our sick leave is used up?" Angela Tremonte said.

"Well, what should we do then?" I asked. "How do we create the conditions necessary for our students to gain a better education when those who want to keep things the way they have always been control all the Queens, Kings, and Aces?"

Chapter 10: 1968

When I returned home after a day-long educational conference about the year 1968, Ana and I sat down with glasses of wine. She asked me what I heard and learned. I said, "Ana, first, and most important for me, I must say I lived a lifetime today."

"Mark, that sounds like a stretch. I need you to explain that to me."

"Affecting me the most during the conference was when the meetings' presenters and participants talked about the assassinations of The Reverend Martin Luther King Jr. in April and Senator Robert F. Kennedy in June of 1968. And if that were not potent enough, another set of presenters debated the Vietnam conflict and its escalation. The third major topic discussed was the presidential election of 1968 and its ramifications. I lived through these events at the time they transpired, and I lived through them again today."

"Sounds like a full day, or as you are suggesting, enough to fill a life."

"Yes, it was a full day that felt like my entire lifespan," I said.

"I believe I understand, Mark. I have had the same experience when an event encompasses a life full of feelings, and I have had several of those. What was it that you heard and learned that has had such a big impact on you?" Ana asked.

"First, Ana, let me start by explaining the highlights from the presentations and the follow-up discussions about the assassinations of New York senator and presidential candidate in 1968, Robert Kennedy, and The Reverend King."

"I am listening," Ana said.

"In those momentous three hundred and sixty-five days of 1968, public events touched every American, including me, a sophomore in college at the time. Fifty-plus years later, nineteen sixty-eight still rouses my heart and mind." I said.

"Because of my situation in those days, I missed a lot of what you must have experienced," Ana said. "So, Honey, please fill me in on what you learned at the conference. Also, tell me about your own experience, as you have indicated, in that fateful year."

"Sure, Ana. During the conference, we discussed a number of issues relevant to you and me and to our students," I said. "Panel speakers informed the audience about the demonstrations in the streets, the assassinations of political leaders, and the angst throughout American society that shook and shaped the citizens experiencing them. Panelists identified the societal trauma occurring over a half century ago and illustrated how the Vietnam conflict's aftermath continues to define those who lived through the era—even to the present day."

"Who attended the conference, Mark?" Ana asked.

"High school and college educators who teach the history of the late 1960's and early 1970's enrolled in the conference, as well as members of the public.

"Several participants first birthdays had not been

celebrated until well after the evacuation of the United States military from Vietnam in April of 1975. Educators and citizens wanted to learn what those who had lived through the events of 1968 had to say.

"The conference attendees who had not been born until after the United States had exited the southeast Asian country, had heard and read about Vietnam and its domestic repercussions. However, they knew little of the trauma their parents and grandparents faced.

"On family trips, some conference registrants had visited the commemorative Vietnam Wall in Washington, D. C. However, to most of the younger attendees, the history of the Vietnam conflict and the anguish surrounding the combat was just that—history. Yet, as I felt when I visited the Wall, the warfare touches and stirs visitors when they trace the inscriptions of the names of those we knew or wish we did."

"Mark, your telling of these events sends shivers throughout my body and mind," Ana said.

"It is emotional for me too," I said.

"I can feel its effect on you," Ana said.

"Yes, indeed. I and the other educators attending the conference wanted to educate more of our students about the historical record, but first we needed to learn the history. Conference presenters struggled to describe the national apprehensiveness through the 1960s and 1970s. Memories seared the emotions of those who had lived through the turmoil. It is difficult to describe in words the era's despair.

"Younger faculty had studied the conflict and the associated societal discord in books and through watching the extant video. However, if they did not live through the upheaval as you and I had, it was hard for young people to understand the time period's poignant intensity.

"Veteran educators and long-time Gorham's citizens I have known for years also attended the conference. We heard from various speakers and audience members about life in 1968. For the first time, most of the younger participants heard fresh testimony.

"For at least a day, a conference about the fateful year of 1968 brought young and old together to experience what some had—and some had not. When sessions were effective, we felt the presenters' passions."

"Overall, Mark, what was the conference trying to accomplish?" Ana asked.

"The conference's goal was to provide educators with information and methodologies in which to teach about 1968's nation-changing events," I said.

"Did you hear about specific events in nineteen sixty-eight, and their impact on society at the time?" Ana asked.

"Yes, the facts of the matter are relatively clear. In the spring of 1968, The Reverend Martin Luther King Jr. traveled to Memphis, Tennessee, to support city sanitation workers who were on strike. On April fourth, an assassin shot Dr. King to death outside his hotel room. The country responded, in some places with violence."

"Do you have any personal memories or testimony of some of what happened around the country after the assassination?" Ana asked.

"Yes, I do. According to a friend of mine who was in New York City at the time, the response to the news in New York was mostly peaceful. As we know from history, however, sections of Washington, DC, burst into flames," I said.

"Mark, in the session about 1968, because you lived through the year's events, did you say anything in the session?" Ana asked.

"Yes, I did. I relayed to the conference the story about my friend who was in New York City at the time The Reverend King was shot in Memphis. Journeying with two roommates, my friend shared with me what the experience was like in the city. I still have the letter in my filing cabinet. I will get it," I said.

"I would like you to read it to me," Ana said.

"Okay. Ana, here is what my friend wrote at the time about what he witnessed, 'Mark, it was surreal. I was in Time's Square shortly after the news of the assassination reached us. The area around the Square fell eerily quiet. It felt like something could happen any moment. We did not see violence break out in the city. Yet, my buddies and I could feel the air's thickness. We stood still not having any idea what might happen next. Eerie silence fell on us and fellow travelers. We saw no violence, but it felt like anything could happen without warning.' That is what he communicated to me about what occurred in New York when my friend was there."

"Mark, at the conference, did they talk about the difference between what happened in New York compared to the fires and damage to property in Washington, DC? I ask this because a cousin of mine living in the District of Columbia told my relatives how frightened she was witnessing the destruction in her neighborhood in April of 1968."

"Yes, conference presenters talked about the different reactions around the United States to the news of Dr. King's death. As your cousin apparently communicated, some Washington, DC residents responded differently to the news of The Reverend King's death than what was happening in New York City. The reaction in New York City was relatively peaceful—Washington, DC was not."

"Mark, that confirms what my cousin told me. What

else did you learn at the conference?" Ana asked.

"There were a couple of panels discussing events in Vietnam. One presenter argued the North Vietnamese 'Tet Offensive' in February of 1968 illustrated to the American public the futility of the fighting in southeast Asia. Based on what we heard in this and other sessions at the conference, the United States had little hope of peacefully extracting itself from the conflict. To make things worse, the government was not telling the truth to the American people."

"I remember hearing newscasts about the difficulties in getting out of the quagmire in Vietnam," Ana said.

"Yes, Ana, at the conference we heard about the problems in extracting ourselves out of the conflict. Panel members said repeatedly that the news of events in Vietnam was not getting out to the American people," I said.

"Looking back, Mark, it is clear we were kept in the fog not knowing what was going on," Ana said.

"Indeed, a full recounting of events in Vietnam was not being imparted to America's citizenry," I said.

"We now know that don't we, Mark?" Ana asked.

"Yes, we do, Ana. Vietnam became a central issue in the 1968 presidential campaign," I responded. "As a result of what was transpiring in Asia, another speaker reported that Senator Eugene McCarthy of Minnesota received enough votes in the New Hampshire presidential preference primary to convince the incumbent president, Lyndon B. Johnson, to withdraw from the contest.

"In March of that year, Johnson's withdrawal transformed the election. Without the sitting president in the campaign, the election opened wide for candidates who had different ideas about the Vietnam conflict, and how to remove ourselves from the morass we could not win and little understood."

"From your report of what you heard at the conference, Mark, it is a gross understatement to say that 1968 was anything but a revolutionary year in the life of the country."

"Yes, Ana, I agree. However, there is more to tell. Shortly after March 31, 1968, when President Johnson said he would not seek re-election to the presidency, New York Senator Robert F. Kennedy entered the presidential contest.

"Then, on June 4, 1968, the evening when Kennedy won the California primary, an assassin shot and killed him in Los Angeles."

"Mark, that is two assassinations of significant people in one year. I remember, although I was still too young to vote, it shook the nation, and it shook me," Ana said.

"Yes, and as if that were not enough, fury broke out at the Democratic convention in Chicago. Demonstrators occupied the streets as the major television networks telecast the bedlam to the rest of the nation. With mixed success, law enforcement tried to control the turmoil in Chicago in the summer of 1968."

"What a year, Mark. It seems so chaotic as I look back," Ana said.

"It was. However, the tumult was nowhere near over. It continued after the Chicago convention. On November 5, 1968, Richard M. Nixon defeated Hubert H. Humphrey to become president of the United States—a presidency terminating in 1974."

"I don't recall the details although I remember Nixon resigned. What did happen?" Ana asked.

"Following the revelation of the political machinations surrounding the break in at the Watergate Hotel, the threat of impeachment proceedings compelled Nixon to resign. Nixon's resignation ended his second term with more than two years remaining."

"This, too, must have shocked the nation—a president resigning!" Ana said.

"Indeed—it sure did. In addition to a presidential resignation in 1968, and further frightening to the establishment, protestors throughout the United States challenged the status quo. The entrenched powers did not like it, and ever since they have been trying to discredit the protests and protestors and what the protesting was all about."

"Have they been successful in their effort to discredit the protestors' message, Mark?"

"Yes, at least in part. For example, one presenter at the conference, Marylyn Frigorie, declared that the industrial giants who make the weapons of war have been partially successful in undermining the anti-war movement spawned in the 1960's. With the election of Ronald Reagan in 1980, Dr. Frigorie argued the weaponized power structure re-gained control. Ever since the Reagan administrations, she contends the conservative political forces have increased their hegemony and dominated politics, and the weapons' manufacturers have continued selling what they have been manufacturing," I said.

"What else did you learn at the conference that educators need to be aware of?" Ana asked.

"The educators in universities and schools need to realize they are being watched," I responded. "The last thing faculty want to happen is to be featured or even citied in the news for teaching their biases. This is especially problematic for those without tenure, but even some tenured professors do not want to be trolled with their comments edited to embarrass them on the World Wide Web for anyone to access.

"Teachers could be cited even in cases when the other

side is given a chance in classes to freely express their views. Conservative views represent the status quo, so those who want to conserve the system are considered safe. Their views can be freely expressed without critique from administrators protecting the system's sources of money."

"Mark, maybe the respective media can help to balance things," Ana said.

"Well, Ana, the usual argument is that the media are liberal and express the viewpoints of the left. One presenter, though, argued that in fact the media are conservative. She contended the networks make money sensationalizing news stories. And, because they profit from the present political and economic system, they want to conserve it."

"So much for receiving unvarnished, unbiased news," Ana said.

"Yup. There is no such thing," I asserted.

"What else did you learn at the conference?" Ana asked.

"In addition to the sessions on the year 1968, there were break-out sessions talking about what occurred in two transitional years, 1958 and 1945. This helped us to comprehend what led to the events of the late sixties and learning about the 1960's helps us to understand today."

"How did they do this in the break-outs?

"Well, Ana, for example, the nineteen fifty-eight panel featured high school graduates from that year. The session illustrated how different 1958 and 1968—just one decade apart—were from each other."

"What did you hear about the class of 1958 that struck you as important?" Ana asked.

"The class of 1958 graduates were the children of the World War II generation," I responded, "Many World

War II families gave birth to children who grew to become protesters against the Vietnam conflict, much to the chagrin of their World War II parents' generation."

"Mark, this conference covered a lot."

"Yes, it did, Ana. Also, I attended a conference seminar in which panelists who lived or studied the years 1945, 1958, and 1968 talked about what took place during those years. A last panelist discussed the counterculture that developed in the 1960s."

"What did you learn from those sessions?" Ana asked.

"Well, we heard from Jim Blazer who was eighteen years old when he joined the army in 1945," I said. "He wheeled into the session with a nurse at his side. Although being along in years, he used his sharp memory of his participation in some of the final events toward the end of World War II to express to us what it was like.

"I have a recording of the panel discussion on the years 1945 and 1958 so I have written down what was said. In the session about 1945, Blazer recounted: 'We fought the war. It was necessary to do so. Japan attacked us at Pearl Harbor. We had no choice but to respond. We also had to drop the bomb on Japan to end the war. I realize that was a controversial decision.'"

"Blazer continued, 'I was away from my family for two years. I was young and lonely. Had it not been for the G. I. Bill, I would have never had the chance to go to college. I did go to college because of government support. I learned a trade at the two-year college I attended.

"When I was overseas, I had infrequent contact with my family. There was no email or available international phone service back then. Also, you had to be careful with whom you communicated and how you did it because of security reasons. As a result, I had little contact with family or friends in the United States, or with anyone outside the military.

"During World War II, I saw buddies shot, some of them grievously. I saw more dead bodies than I ever want to see again. I saw some things and did some things that I am not proud of. It was wartime—hideous killing and maiming stays with you forever.

"To this day, I have trouble attending open-casket funerals. And, at my age I have attended way too many memorial services. This is all I am going to say about the war itself because I get too emotional even thinking about it. I have had many sleepless nights pondering what happened when I was over there. I have already said too much about the action.

"So, to go on—The GI Bill provided access to the training that has enabled me to attain a good job and raise my children—all of whom have gone to college. A pension and social security have provided my wife and me enough money to live. Medicare has helped us obtain the medical care we need. Over the past few years, we have been able to live the good life.

"In 1950, I joined a country club which allowed me to enjoy the outdoors with my friends. I was even able to get my golf handicap under ten. We bought a small mobile home on the South Carolina coast and had many good times with our golfing friends.

"We drank in backyard parties—sometimes too much—but we didn't hurt anyone, or at least I hope we didn't. We enjoyed barbecues with new and old friends. This was the good life—then it crashed into the Cold War. I thought we fought the second world war so we would have world peace. So, I asked myself, 'What in hell is going on?'

"We didn't want other nations leading us into any more trouble. We had fought wars in the world to end wars. We were ready to party and make babies.

"However, we didn't want any trouble from rebellious children. We believed our kids should go to school, get good grades, behave themselves, get married, move to little houses in the suburbs, then into bigger houses when they could afford to, and not ask us for any more money. We had done our part. We believed the world would be peaceful because we had fought the good fight. It was time for others to make the world safe for democracy.

"However, our dreams have been dashed. The world is not what we fought for. I will end here and turn the microphone over to Randy who will talk about the year 1958."

"Thank you, Jim. Hello, my name is Randy Barer. I graduated from high school in 1958. I will talk about what being in the class of 1958 was like, and what life in and out of school was like in the late 1950's.

"Well, we had rock and roll, and we had Elvis. Our parents and older relatives lived through World War II, but that was already a distant memory for youth a decade plus after the atomic bomb ended the war. In the late fifties, we were having seemingly endless fun.

"In the decade of the 1950s, there was a lack of commitment. However, we began to realize that the hot wars of the 1940s had turned cold in the fifties. The prospect of a nuclear conflagration emerged to the forefront of our thinking. In the next decade—the 1960s we have already discussed—many of us would be involved in fighting in Vietnam. Others from the class of 1958 demonstrated their objections to the conflict in Southeast Asia. Also, many of us in the class of 1958 were no longer complacent. We became active—some of us by fighting in Vietnam—others by protesting the fighting."

"Panel member, Tammy Wirre, spoke about the class of 1968. She said, 'Other panels and speakers have already discussed 1968 when all hell broke loose. We thought all could be lost and was being lost. I was one of those protesters we all read and hear about today. I was out to change things. I lived in a commune with others. Yes, there was sex and some drugs—more sex than drugs. I hear some laughter. I am simply trying to tell those of you here today who did not live through that period what it was like, at least for me. Some of you may remember unless you too were too high to recall.'"

"After more crowd laughter, Tammy Wirre continued, 'In the late 1960's, we thought change was necessary and expected it would come in a hurry. We had our 'Hippies' and counter-culture types. Loud, beating music moved us. The movies challenged the culture in the United States. *Avante garde* books provoked thought and discussion.'"

"'Here we are today—more than fifty years after we graduated. In 1968, we longed for a better future. We are still hoping.' Tammy concluded."

"Ana, this is my report to you about the lifetime I lived during the conference. I realize this has been a long story, but an important one I trust," I said.

"It is important, Mark. I wish I had been there to listen and learn along with you. Our history teaches us a lot. I need to pay more attention," Ana said.

"We all do, Ana. We all do."

Chapter 11: Core

During one of our Friday night dinners, we discussed what the adoption of the Common Core would mean for our classrooms. In attendance were our usual participants: Bailey T. S. Memorial High School social studies and media literacy teacher, Lacey Walsh; Bailey High social studies teachers, Angela Tremonte, John Browne, Charles Yates, Jake Spanner, and Zack Barber; Cheryl Wattsen, chair of the English department in Bailey High School; Bailey High art teacher, Karla Betts; Gorham Central Elementary School teacher, April Danniels; Ana and me.

Jake opened the discussion, "What is this Common Core all about anyway?"

Zack Barber responded, "Forty-two state boards of education, through the authority of their respective state legislatures, have adopted provisions for the implementation of the Common Core in the public schools in their states. Those are the facts. What it means for our classrooms is another matter."

"Not too many people know what the impact of the adoption of the Core will have in practice," I said. "State legislatures passed the Common Core without much educator participation. Few of the legislators who voted for the Core are or have been classroom teachers. We should have been paying more attention. Hopefully, it is not too late to influence national and state education policy."

"In explaining the background, let me add to Zack's comment that the states adopting the Common Core believe the fifty states should have similar objectives for all their students," Cheryl Wattsen said. "The National Governors Association and the Chief State School Officers recommended the Core's passage and copyrighted its content. The two organizations believed the Core would strengthen education throughout the country by requiring similar expectations for students regardless of where in the United States they live and attend school."

"I agree with the Common Core concept as Cheryl explained it. The idea is to prepare all students for college or a career after high school. This is something I am in favor of, and I would think the rest of you would and should be too," Charles Yates said.

"But, Charles, favoring a federal program is unusual for you and more than a bit hypocritical, don't you think? Just because it conforms to your philosophy doesn't make it right," Jake Spanner said.

"And, Charles, I did not say I am in favor of everything in in the Common Core. I was just explaining what the authors of the Core want it to do," Cheryl said.

"Cheryl, what do you see as the downside?" Charles asked.

"Well, for example, I am against the possibility that students will read less fiction," Cheryl said. "I am a strong believer in students reading good literature to improve their reading, writing, and thinking. The Common Core does not include enough good options for reading novels and short stories. Fiction can spark and generate a student's imagination. In addition, stories reveal truths about the human condition and the society we live in, often expressing human qualities beyond what nonfiction can."

"Ana has already examined the Common Core concentrating on its implications for elementary school students. She also studied how the Core affects second language learners. Ana, what have you discovered?" I asked.

"Well, Mark, and everyone, the Common Core has mostly English authors rather than writers from other cultures. What bothers me the most is that the 'Core' is classic Anglo cultural supremacy," Ana said.

"Ana, please explain that further. What are you objecting to?" Cheryl asked.

"I believe all cultures and those other than our own should be respected," Ana said. "By reading books by and about us as well as other cultures, our humanity emerges and is valued. Therefore, we learn to appreciate those who are different.

"The Common Core appears to consider my multiracial culture as the 'other,' or in my case, the 'others.' Not the others we should learn about, but those who are not in the mainstream of White America. We are segregated—if not legally—de facto separated. The Common Core is not about me nor does it reflect people like me. We and many others are isolated and placed outside the dominant Anglo-Saxon culture and its mandated curriculum."

"Ana, I agree. The Core promotes a one-way culture as we once again get sent on the white folk's cultural highway," John Browne said. "There are a whole lot of us who are not included in the Common Core's commonweal. That includes you and me and a whole lot of others who are different from the dominant ethnic ethos."

"I hear what you are saying John. I get it and agree with you," Angela Tremonte said.

"It is never too late to challenge the Core. If the white supremacy dominance is required in the classroom, then it will have a big impact—a negative one. That matters to our students, and I believe should matter to us as faculty," Zack said.

"I agree with questioning the implementation of the Core. There is still time to challenge the standards and that we are mandated to teach to it. I do not consider the requirement good for our students, for us, or for our society. So, we need to question and change it," Ana said.

"It is not a curriculum though is it? Isn't it more a set of goals or objectives like *Bloom's Taxonomy*?" Jake said.

"Yah. That is the problem. It really is nothing new, but they have sent us in a tizzy about it. Once again, people who have little knowledge of what we do in the classroom are trying to tell us what to do. Whether they know anything or not, those who know the least about teaching and learning get to say the most. The authorities set the rules, and teachers are bound to follow the policies of those ignoramuses who have the power," Zack said.

"If it is the law, then we have to follow it. So, we have gotten ourselves into more than just a 'tizzy' as you have labeled it, Zack. The Common Core will affect us all, and I think for the good," Charles Yates insisted. "We need to follow the law and do what the various state boards are telling us to do."

"Charles, you are for following what the government says to do when you agree with the mandates," Ana said. "When you don't agree with federal policy then it is a different story. Isn't that the case?"

"That is right, Ana. I follow those principles I agree with and resist those I dispute. However, I obey the law, even when I oppose some of what I am told to do that go against my beliefs. What is wrong with that?" Charles asked.

"What kind of a society will we have if we only observe those laws and societal principles we agree with?" Cheryl said. "Charles, it is really strange to me that you now want to follow the Common Core."

"Yes, that is right, Cheryl. I believe the Common Core is a good law and should be followed. I advocate changing the laws I disagree with. If you disagree with something, you should all campaign for changes and press legislators to enact better laws, and that also goes for the Common Core. Besides, I bet, Cheryl, you only follow requirements you agree with."

"Oh, Charles. Come on. Once again, you are pushing it. Where is Megan when we need her? She would straighten you out," Jake said.

"Sorry, Jake. Megan Straffa could not 'straighten' me out, as you put it, when she was here in Bailey High. If she were still teaching in Bailey High, Megan would not be able to convince me to abandon my principles. She never did change my mind, and what she advocated while in Bailey High should not change other minds either. I believe Megan's claims lacked evidence and common sense," Charles said.

"What if your beliefs are not good for students, Charles?" Jake asked.

"Oh, come on, Jake. My views are good for the students, and the Common Core is good for our students which is why I favor it," Charles said.

"Charles, you are a propagator, and Megan is an educator," John Browne said.

"Sorry, John, it is the other way around," Charles

snapped back.

"I think you are wrong about what you are saying is good for students, Charles. Your views are just flat out wrong," John retorted.

"We will see, won't we? We will see," Charles responded.

"Yes, we will. But the problem is that by the time we see, as you put it, the Common Core will have bored a lot of students. Furthermore, teachers will have lost valuable instructional time," April Danniels said.

"Once again, it is the elementary teacher who can see what is ahead for students as they proceed through the education system, and whether the Core makes sense for them," Cheryl said.

"Angela Tremonte, you haven't said much in our potluck dinners yet. Do you have something you want to add?" I asked.

"Yes, I do. Megan Straffa left me in charge of the 'keep Charles's propagating under control group.' So, let me say this—Charles Yates—you are all wet. You have never seen or heard a liberal idea you have liked. The fact that you think the Common Core is a good idea makes me suspicious of the whole idea of the Core."

"Go on Angela, I am listening—just like I used to listen to Megan." Charles said smirking.

"Well, Charles, here are just some of the reasons the Common Core is a good and a bad idea. Take your pick," Angela said.

"I am listening," Charles said.

"Okay, Charles and everyone, here goes the argument for: The Core is advocating everyone in the country should be learning the same skills and knowledge base. The skills developed in learning subject matter should be the same for students in every state. As a result, students everywhere would gain the same knowledge base rather than knowledge reserved for the privileged and less knowledge for those without advantages," Angela said. "How am I doing?"

"Fine so far, Angela. Pretty convincing I would say. What then is the argument against?" Charles asked.

"The argument against the Core is the following: Everyone is different; therefore, education for each student should be adapted to the respective learner's style of learning," Angela said. "The various states spend different amounts on each student, so standardizing the outcomes would work against the students in those states which have fewer resources available to spend on their students. Consequently, those who have less will get less and the standardized test scores will most likely be lower for those already disadvantaged. Finally, Charles, the Core will homogenize students in a society in which we need individuality and leadership. Knowing your political views, it seems to me that would be something you are for."

"I hear what you are saying," Charles said.

"Which side are you on then, Charles?" Angela asked.

"I am for the Core, dear Angela. I am for the Core, and the rest of you can manage the best you can."

"Oh, Charles, you are impervious, insufferable, and resistant to progressive change."

"Yes, I probably am what you assert to people like you. However, I like myself the way I am. So, Angela, you would be a better educator and person if you were more like me," Charles said grinning.

"Oh, Charles, you are—indeed—beyond the pale and absolutely irredeemable."

"Thank you, Angela. That is the nicest thing you have ever said to me."

Chapter 12: Shooter

"You have got to be kidding. They are going to train us in a teacher's workshop to do what?" John Browne asked.

"Shoot, and—if need be—shoot to kill," I said.

After we heard about the proposed workshop, our Friday night dinner discussion group decided to talk about what we could expect in the upcoming session.

The possibility of a student or other attacker with a loaded gun in Bailey High was something we loathed to think or talk about, but we knew we had to. A spate of shootings in schools in various communities throughout the United States necessitated the discussion.

Our potluck get-together included: Cheryl Wattsen, English teacher, and chair of the department in Bailey High School; high school art teacher, Karla Betts; Gorham Central Elementary School teacher, April Danniels; high school social studies and media literacy teacher, Lacey Walsh; and Bailey social studies teachers, John Browne, Angela Tremonte, Charles Yates, Jake Spanner, and Zack Barber. Ana and I completed our group.

"Mark, why are they going to conduct mandatory training so we can fight against an active shooter?"

Jake asked as our meeting began.

"Jake, because there have been shootings in schools around the country, so the Board of Education in Gorham, Massachusetts, wants us to be ready if something happens?" I said.

"Mark, what is it the administration wants us to do?" Karla asked incredulously.

"They are directing us to act should there be a shooter in any of our schools. We are being advised to turn off the lights in the classroom. For some students, the darkness would be frightening enough—add a shooter to the dark and we would all be traumatized," I responded.

"We, as teachers, are unprepared for all of this," John Browne said. "What else are they telling us to do in the case of an attack?"

"They are telling us that we should barricade the classroom door, pull shades down, stay away from windows, roll into a fetal position, and remain motionless," I said.

"Geesus, Mark, you don't sound or look like you are joking about 'if something happens.' Assuming you are not joking, then this is terrifying and a new role for us as teachers," Cheryl said.

"I am not joking—and the training IS meant to sound an alarm," I said.

"Hey everyone, I won't carry a gun and I definitely will not work in a school in which teachers are walking around with weapons of any sort used to kill," Karla said.

"Oh, come on, Karla, you sound like Megan Straffa before she left Bailey High. I hope she is smarter now, although I doubt it. Karla, you have been known to care deeply about your students. You want to protect your students, don't you?" Charles Yates challenged.

"Of course, Charles, I do. But that is not the point,"

Karla responded.

"What is the point then, Karla? Squishy-headed liberals like Megan are against guns. I hope you are not one of those who are against using guns for protection and self-defense. Armed teachers can protect our students. You are for us defending ourselves and our students, aren't you?" Charles said.

"Darn it, Charles, you are exaggerating again and misrepresenting my position. Your position is an extreme one," Karla said.

"I am not exaggerating or extreme at all, Karla. You are the extremist if you are against people holding firearms to defend themselves. Is that your position?" Charles asked.

"Once again, Charles, you are distorting what I am saying. I am against teachers carrying guns in school. That is what I am against," Karla responded.

"Maybe so, but the Second Amendment to the *Constitution of the United States* says we have a right to protect ourselves. So, my position is not extreme because it is embedded in the *Constitution*. I think you will agree that our governing document which includes a Bill of Rights is a conservative one, not 'extremist' as you suggest. YOU are the extremist if you are against the Second Amendment as added to the *Constitution of the United States*."

"Charles, you are always retreating to the Second Amendment. I disagree with your interpretation of the amendment. Guns in the hands of people who are untrained on how to use them add another danger to our students and to us. There are too many guns in the United States owned by people who have not undergone background checks or training in gun safety and what they should be used for. We need more gun control in this country—not less. Gun control will help save people's lives—not guns in the hands of teachers," Jake said.

"Jake and everyone, I am not alone on this. Zack agrees with me. Don't you, Zack?" Charles asked.

"Yes, Charles, I do agree with you. No one should tell me, a Libertarian, that I can't and shouldn't protect myself," Zack said.

"Jake and Karla and the rest of the liberals in this group, I believe you need to read and understand the amendment. It will help you appreciate a basic right we have in the United States. Zack seems to understand what our rights are. So, as I said, the Second Amendment to the *Constitution of the United States* allows for gun ownership. You all are trying to restrict our Constitutional rights, and you are wasting our time even talking about it," Charles said.

"Charles, I don't like the condescending tone directed at me and others who don't accept your interpretation of the alleged Constitutional protection for gun ownership without restrictions. I am sure the Second Amendment does not advocate teachers and students carrying guns to school. Does it?" Karla said.

"No, it does not say that specifically. However, the *Constitution* does not prohibit it. Therefore, it implicitly allows the carrying of guns, especially by authorized persons, who in this case would be teachers. I believe it should be legally and administratively permitted for teachers and administrators to carry guns for defensive purposes in schools," Charles responded.

"Let me get into this," Lacey Walsh insisted. "In addition to debating the issues Charles and Karla have identified, there is another issue for all of us to consider besides teachers carrying guns."

"What is it Lacey?" I asked.

"Well, there is an agency talking about training

students to patch shooting victims' wounds. The idea is that students would repair wounds after a shooting," Lacey said.

"Ugh. In addition, Lacey, some people have argued that students should carry bullet-proof backpacks," Angela Tremonte said.

"What? I hope this time the two of you are joking, but I am afraid you aren't," Jake said.

"Jake, Lacey and I am not joking about something this serious," Angela said.

"So, now we have additional trauma for our students—carrying first- aid kits with bullet-proof backpacks. What are we coming to?" Ana asked, incredulous.

"Yah, Ana, fear can drive us to some dangerous solutions. Solutions that will lead us to become even more frightened thinking about what might happen—I emphasize 'might,'" Lacey said.

"What is the alternative, Lacey? Do you have one?" Charles asked.

"We need to work at preventing violence in the first place. This whole issue of guns in our society and violence in general is a societal problem—not one we should assign to our students to solve. Instead of doing what we as educators should do—prevent violence—we are putting the burden on the students to save themselves," Lacey said.

"And, because we have no plan in place to stop any potential shooting before it starts, it is absurd that we as faculty must learn how to shoot to stop the shooters—that would just be reactive and can easily result into a gunfight with bullets sprayed throughout classrooms and school corridors," Jake Spanner said.

"Jake, are you and the other liberals in this group against saving our students?" Charles asked.

"Oh, come on, Charles, don't be ridiculous. You are

once again stretching things way out of proportion. You are trying to turn things around. Your debating strategy will not work on me or the rest of us. Of course, we are for keeping students safe. The question is—what is the best way to do that?" Jake asked.

"Sorry, Jake. What we have been doing in schools has not worked—has it? We would not be talking about this issue if the status quo were working. People with guns are killing students around the country. What are we going to do about it?" Charles asked.

"Not what you think we ought to do, Charles. Arming teachers and instructing how to shoot is not the answer. Is that what you are for—teaching all teachers how to shoot—to shoot to kill? Am I right about that?" Cheryl asked.

"Yes, Cheryl, and everyone—that is what I think we ought to do. We should train teachers how to shoot to protect themselves and their students," Charles asserted. "And, if necessary, to kill to save lives."

"I am completely against what you are advocating, Charles," Karla stated.

"What do you think we ought to do then, Karla? Are you recommending we do nothing? Is that what you propose we do—just stand aside and watch the shooter kill our colleagues and our students?" Charles asked.

"Charles, of course, that is not what I want. As usual, when we disagree, you twist my words. I believe whatever we do should not include teachers carrying guns in school." Karla said.

"How about the idea of students carrying bullet-proof backpacks? Karla, you and the rest of this group must be for protective backpacks to shield the kids, aren't you?" Charles said.

"Charles, you are being absurd," Karla said.

"What do we do then to protect the students?" Charles

asked.

“Keep guns out of the schools,” Karla stated.

“Well, I get your point about keeping guns out of school. However, Jake, Karla, and everyone, what are you going to do if someone or more than one potential killer enters our school with a gun or guns intent on murdering our students? Are you going to allow students to die?” Charles challenged.

“No one is for anyone in our school getting hurt. However, teachers carrying guns in school will not solve the problem,” Cheryl said.

“On the contrary, Cheryl, I believe we need to provide teachers with guns in the classroom to save lives. With guns, we can defend our students and ourselves. We should also provide bullet-proof backpacks to our students for protection,” Charles said.

“I don’t think the idea of arming teachers will help at all. Charles, it won’t solve anything, and the backpacks will not save anyone when the gunshots are flying everywhere,” Cheryl said.

“I totally agree with Cheryl,” Karla said.

“Karla, I continue to be shocked you are against using guns to protect our students and ourselves,” Charles said sarcastically.

At that point in the discussion, I had to intervene because of the late hour. “Unfortunately, we have to call it a night. Ana and I have a morning appointment tomorrow. We certainly do not have an agreement on how we should proceed to protect our students and ourselves, or what we could recommend to school administrators. Do we?” I said.

“No, we don’t, Mark—no we don’t!” Charles stressed.

“Well, Charles, we finally found something we agree on,” Karla said.

“What is that, Karla?” Charles asked.

"We agree —we don't have an agreement," Karla stated.

"Yes, we agree that we don't agree. Therefore, what are we going to do when there has been another shooter killing indiscriminately in a school? We grow criminality in this country, and the killers may be coming after us and our students here in Bailey. We need to be ready for that eventuality—if it comes to that—and the way things are going in the United States and around the world, it just might," Charles said.

"Charles, you identified what may be THE problem—'we grow' people who are willing to use any means necessary to get what they want and hurt other people," John Browne said. "We need to find out why this happens and how to deal with it. Teachers with guns will not solve the problem."

"What will work, John?" Charles asked.

"We will have to educate our society out of the need to use weapons to solve problems."

"I get your point, John, but that will take a while," Charles said. "So, in the interim, let me state again the relevant and immediate question: What do we do if someone with a gun walks into Bailey T. S. Memorial High School intending to do us and our students harm, and the perpetrator starts spraying bullets all over the place? What do we do then—just duck?"

"Oh, Charles, you are being ridiculous," Cheryl said.

"So, Cheryl, I repeat:

"What do you propose we do in the event of someone with evil intent walking through this school with a gun loaded with ammunition?" Charles asked. "What is it that you and the rest of our faculty recommend?"

Chapter 13: Fake v. News

"A number of people are using the terminology 'fake news.' However, using that term is misleading. If it is fake, it is not news," Lacey Walsh said at the beginning of one of our potluck dinners.

Because she had been in the television industry, we listened intently when Lacey spoke about televised news and news delivery in general.

The potluck dinner included in attendance our usual group of Angela Tremonte, John Browne, Lacey Walsh, Charles Yates, Jake Spanner, Zack Barber, Cheryl Wattsen, April Danniels, Karla Betts, Ana, and me.

"This is important for us to know about," I said. "Please tell us more."

"Okay, Mark. If everyone wants me to, I will," Lacey said.

"Yes, we are interested," The dinner group said in unison.

"So, here goes. In addition to dissembling and employing distraction through the various media, propagators use verbal manipulation designed to confuse us and our students. For example, language manipulators confuse listeners through comments such as, 'He probably didn't do it, and even if he did, it is okay, but he could have or he could not have;' or, 'He may have done it, but probably didn't.' With assertions like these, readers, listeners, and viewers do not know what someone is saying, or which side they are on. Rather than to inform, such statements are meant to confuse and distract. The propagators succeed all too often. We should help our students decipher linguistic sleights of hand," Lacey said.

"Is that the intent of such language, I mean, to bamboozle?" Jake asked with quizzical smile on his face.

"Yes, it is. If the view generated is that nothing is true, then the manipulator can fill the vacuum with one's own version of the truth. Propagandists trade in confusion, cynicism, and doubt," Lacey said.

"Yikes. Damn it, Lacey, this stuff works all too often on us, our students, and on the public in general," Jake said.

"Yes, it does. Jake and everyone, I am afraid it does work on us and our students if we are ill-prepared to discern truth from fiction. Furthermore, social media is generating all kinds of disinformation and misinformation," Lacey said. "As educators in the increasingly complex and complicated world we all live in, Bailey High faculty need to help students learn how to determine what is true and what is not—not an easy task with contemporary technology. When visuals accompany misleading language, then the incomplete visual syllogisms can convince us that up is down and down is up unless we and our students are discriminant visually and literally."

"I believe, indeed, there is a war on truth. We as teachers need to be truth-seekers and help our students find out what is true so they can be good citizens and truth-tellers," Zack Barber said. "Lacey, this goes beyond what you have taught us before about media literacy, doesn't it?"

"Yes, Zack, it does. The propagators are gaining in sophistication, and new technologies enable transmission of fraudulent communications," Lacey responded.

"Lacey, how then do we help students and even ourselves identify what is true and what isn't?" I asked.

"As I mentioned in a previous workshop, when I was in the television news business, we basically sold viewers' eyeballs to advertisers," Lacey said. "It was believed to be a fair deal—we received the advertisers' dollars and they acquired customers who bought their products. The ads were designed to convince viewers to buy products and services, and just about anything goes when lots of dollars can be made. Whether ideas or products, propagators use whatever means at their disposal necessary to sell and coax people to buy."

"How do they get away with the falsification, Lacey?" Angela Tremonte asked.

"There are a variety of ways to shape the message and generate false information. Under closer examination, what appears factual may not be. Educators and news professionals are now using the terminology—fake news. Although, as I have already said, if it is fake then it is not news. More apt terms would be misinformation, disinformation, and propaganda."

"I need an explanation. The allegation that there are fabricators intentionally faking news is bizarre. This all sounds too cynical even for me," Charles Yates said.

"Yes. I realize it may sound that way," Lacey said. "However, I believe that is the way it is, and students need to be informed on how news producers work."

"So, what do schools need to do?" I asked.

"Mark and everyone, this is what I believe students need to know to have a chance to be informed," Lacey continued. "We, as teachers, can help students understand how news producers gather, produce, and deliver the news, and that all media are not the same. Reading the newspaper is quite a different experience than watching a television screen. When reading, you must think to gain meaning. Furthermore, when reading, the reader is in control and can stop and think before going on. This is not the case when watching fast moving images. The propagator uses moving images to drop in messages to those who are not media literate.

"As teachers, I believe we should discuss with students what they have read, seen, and experienced. In the twenty first century, this practice is the heart of becoming an educated person."

"Lacey, are you advocating we integrate what you are proposing throughout the curriculum?"

"Yes, absolutely. Media literacy in all of its permutations should be part of what we teach in every course of study." Lacey said.

"That is a tall order, Lacey," I said.

"Yes, it is, Mark. But we live in this increasingly technological world with multifaceted ways to manipulate the public. As a result, students need to learn how to critically view what they see in the visual media, critically think about what they hear, and read print with critical eyes."

Chapter 14: Work

"Mr. M., my family works hard for what we have. Why should other people be on welfare and get things they are not working for?" Elena asked in my "Current Issues" social studies class.

"What do you mean, Elena, when you use the word work?" I asked.

"You must know what I mean—Work, W-O-R-K, work! You know, Mr. M.—WORK," Elena responded.

"I get what you are saying, but I need to have you explain what YOU mean by work," I said.

"Are you sure you need me to do that, Mr. M.? You are college- educated and must know what work means," Elena said with a sigh.

"I want you to do the best you can to tell me and the class what you, Elena, mean by work."

"Well, Mr. M., I am getting frustrated. I know what I mean—maybe someone else in class can tell you what work is. I am surprised you don't know," Elena said with her voice trailing off.

"Yah, Mr. M., what do you mean by work? To me, Elena, and I bet others in class, it is obvious what work is," Mickie said.

"Mickie, Elena, and everyone, I have my own

definition. I would like to hear what you and your classmates mean when you say work," I said.

"You are always asking us to define terms. Why don't you just give us the answer if you know what it means?" Kenny said.

"If I tell you, Kenny, then thinking stops. You would then have the teacher's answer, not necessarily the right answer, and certainly not your answer."

"Hey, Mr. M., we students have always been told that what the teacher tells us is always right. Are you saying that teachers are wrong sometimes?" Ronnie inquired with a skeptical grimace.

"Yes, Ronnie, teachers are wrong on occasion. So, the teacher's answer isn't always the correct or complete one," I said.

"I am glad you admit that," Kenny said to laughter. "Anyway, it takes a lot longer to learn stuff this way—you know—when we have to think about it ourselves."

"I hear what you are saying, but I want to hear what you come up with as you think about terminology—in this case the word 'work.' So, if someone could define it for the rest of us, I and the rest of the class are listening," I said.

"Mr. M., how did you come up with this way of teaching? My uncle had you as a teacher when you first started teaching. He said you lectured more back then."

"Kenny, you are right about that. I did lecture more back then. At the beginning of my teaching career, I taught the way I had been taught. However, I later learned from a great teacher we had here years ago. His name was Ken Lewiston. We called him Mr. K. I learned from him that you as students must think for yourselves to learn. I discovered I could not and should not do the thinking for you. Mr. K. was expert at stimulating thinking through asking questions. I am trying to do some of the same kind of questioning he did. For me, he was a role model of what a teacher should be."

"Hey, Kenny, that teacher Mr. M. learned from has your first name, maybe he was your father," Curtis said to laughter.

"Okay, okay, back to the issue," I said.

"Alright, Mr. M., here is my definition of work," Curtis said.

"I am listening, Curtis," I said.

"Work is doing something productive. Yah, that is it," Curtis responded.

"Studying is productive, which according to your definition would make it a job. Isn't that right?" I asked.

"Maybe so, but we don't get paid, so it isn't a real job," Daryl quipped.

"However, Daryl, if you study and then get a job because of what you learned then you will get paid for studying because gaining knowledge eventually enabled you to receive money for working," I said.

"You get paid just because you study. I don't think so, Mr. M," Daryle responded.

"I believe through studying you will gain employment and get you paid for the quality of work you do," I said.

"How so, Mr. M.?" Bettina asked.

"Well, Bettina, you don't necessarily have to study to get a job—you can get a job without studying. On the other hand, if you study and know something or how to accomplish certain tasks then I believe you will get paid because of what you studied and learned. Further study, resulting in improving the quality of your work, helps you to stay employed and get promoted. Promotions generally lead to a higher salary."

"Are you sure about all of that, Mr. M.?" Marena asked.

"As sure as I can be, and I believe there is evidence

to support the contention—the more education, the greater chance for employment and at a higher level of pay," I said.

"Would you call what you do, work?" Margaret asked.

"Yes, I would. I obtained an education, prepare for class, and then try to help you learn the subject matter," I responded.

"Not very laborious I would say," Sandy said.

"Sandy, and everyone, it all depends on how you look at it. So, back to defining work. Most of the time we work to earn money. However, work is defined in different ways. For example, I characterize getting prepared for class as working," I said.

"A lot of people, Mr. M., would not define what you do as work," Annita said to laughter.

"I realize that, and I realize work means different things to different people," I replied.

"Yah, I am ready to work and make money. I want to make a lot of money, but I do not want to work too hard. I want a job like yours where I do not have to work too hard. However, I would want to make a lot more money than you do," Manny said to more laughter.

"Okay, Mr. M., now that we are defining terms, what does the 'hard' part mean when we talk about working?" Sandy asked.

"What does it mean when people say 'hard' work, or working hard? Sandy, is that what you are asking?" I asked.

"Yes. Mr. M., that is what I am asking," Sandy replied.

"Okay, Sandy and everyone. How would you define hard work?" I asked.

"Mr. M., you are always turning the questions back on us," Edwin said.

"That is part of my job—my work—asking questions to stimulate further thought. So, Edwin, how would you define hard work and studying in particular?" I asked.

"I would not call studying hard work. It isn't like cleaning people's houses and lifting heavy objects—which is real work," Edwin said.

"Or having a job doing pick and shovel," Sanford added.

"Is the definition of hard work the hours you put in, or how hard you work during those hours?" I asked.

"Both," Camron said.

"So, when people say, 'work hard,' what do they mean?" I asked.

"We are going in circles Mr. M. We do that sometimes in this class," Michael said.

"Maybe we are returning to a previous question we thought was settled but wasn't. It is difficult to get anywhere in a discussion unless we define terms, agree on those definitions, and then delineate exactly what we mean and are talking about," I said.

"Mr. M., what we are doing in class today is hard work," Ramon said.

"Why do you say that, Ramon?" I asked.

"Because we have to think," Ramon responded.

"So, hard work does not have to be physical. Is that what you are saying?" I asked.

"Yes. Not only is thinking hard work, but we are not earning any money in class today. So, we are 'working' but not getting paid. So, working and money are not connected sometimes," Emanuel stated.

"Yes, although learning through studying and thinking might lead to employment and a good salary later in life," I said.

"Mr. M., thinking is hard work. So, I am beginning to believe hard work could be either physical or mental, or it could be both at the same time," Ellenna said.

"How about being emotionally invested in something.

Can that be hard work?" I asked.

"Yes. If mental and physical activity can be defined as hard work, then I guess emotional involvement can too," Anthony said.

"From what I hear you all saying, there are a lot of ways to define work. Is that what those of you who have commented today are saying?" I asked.

"I guess that is what we are saying. We are going to have to think about this stuff, Mr. M.," Elena said. "I am a little confused at the moment, or a lot confused actually."

"I hope we all think about what we have been discussing regarding what work is, defining our terms and so forth," I said.

"That includes you too, doesn't it, Mr. M.?" Alessa said.

"Yes, it sure does. I am learning all the time, and you get me to re-think concepts that I have thought to be true and settled in my mind. When you offer counter ideas to what I believe, I find I need to re-examine some things I thought I knew and then revise previous concepts. So, thanks to all of you. Your comments challenge some of my previous conclusions forcing me to make them into hypotheses to be tested before I can conclude," I responded.

"Glorie, you want to say something."

"Yes, I do, Mr. M. Some day you will have to expand on what you just said about hypotheses. What I want to say though relates to the question of what work is. My father works two jobs, and both are hard labor. Also, my aunt cleans people's houses. Those jobs are real work," Glorie said.

"You have a point there, Glorie. There are different kinds of work. Depending on how you define it, some work is much harder physically than other kinds of work. Do we agree on that?" I asked.

"Sort of, Mr. M. I believe work involving our emotions and mental work can be hard work too," Opala asserted.

"Opala, you have given the class something else to think about," I said.

"Mr. M., how about this for us to think about? What do you and members of the class believe about those people who for one reason or another don't or won't do any kind of work—physical or otherwise?" Dennis asked.

"Yes, Mr. M., what should we do about those people?" Frederica asked.

"Well, Dennis and Frederica, the bell is about to ring, so let me leave the class with the following—think about the issues of work, hard work, and what those terms mean. Also, please give some thought to the issue Dennis and Frederica just raised. I mean about those who, as the two of you have defined it, 'do not or will not work.' What should our society do in those cases?"

"That is easy, Mr. M.—let them starve," Ramon said to groans.

"You can't do that, Ramon," Frederica countered as class was about to end.

"Oh, yes, I can. And there are others in this class who agree with me," Ramon responded as the students began gathering their belongings.

"Okay, you all will need to go on to your next class shortly. Have we arrived at a consensus?" I said.

"No, I don't believe we have Mr. M.—not even close," Angie said.

"I agree with Angie, not even close to a consensus," Jasmin said.

"Keep thinking then. Keep thinking," I urged.

"Mr. M., it hurts my head to think so much," Antin said.

"Why don't we just work and let the government or

you, Mr. M., do the thinking about everything for us so we can just make money and live our lives?" Alfonse said.

"What do the rest of you think about Alfonse's idea?" I asked as the bell rang.

"I certainly don't agree with Alphonse. We are nowhere near agreement on this. And, Mr. M., we haven't determined what a hypothesis is," Glorie said.

Chapter 15: "Go Home!"

"Go home." A few of my students heard this directive when they walked Gorham's streets.

As more immigrants moved into Gorham, anti-immigrant locals hurled insults at school-aged children and their parents. Invectives accompanied the demands to get out of Gorham and "go back to where you came from and stay there."

The dictates to go back to where they came from frightened students who had settled with family members in this New England town. The families and their children hoped for a better life through education in Gorham's schools. Instead, some encountered harassment in their search for learning.

Through its history, Gorham, Massachusetts, affirmed its Caucasian identity. The community's elite preferred it remain that way. The message sent to those new settlers considered "foreign" was to "go away."

Those who were different from Gorham's natives could work for the property owners if buses brought them in from other communities. The implicit agreement was that the workers returned to "where they belonged" at the end of the workday, or at dark—whichever came first.

Self-selected Gorham citizens wanted to continue busing workers into town so the community would remain as it had always been. However, when Gorham annexed adjacent communities to increase its tax base, immigrants in larger numbers began attending Gorham's schools. Epithets all too frequently greeted the new Bailey High students and their family members. Several new families with school-age children were told to "get out of town or else."

Red paint plastered on a living room wall of their ransacked home told a family to "GO AWAY!" A phone message on the family's recorder advised, "Don't sleep at night. If you do, you won't see your flaming garage explode."

Ringing doorbells at midnight awakened families. When the occupants opened the door to see who was there—floodlights blinded eyes. To accent the message, hackers captured homeowners' technologies to tell occupants, "WE SEE YOU."

In a community adjacent to Gorham, rapists painted a message in purple on a molested woman's chest, "If you do not get out of town, foreigners like you deserve what you get and will get more of it. Hey, by the way—WATCH YOUR KIDS."

The question of who belonged in Gorham bedeviled the town's citizenry. Bailey High's staff tried to welcome everyone who attended. Influential town residents balked.

In attempts to denigrate people who came from other nations, racists employed various forms of insult. Published cartoons, some distorting black and brown faces, attempted to reinforce that in Gorham the "lily-white preferred." The cryptic message, "you are not wanted except to work in this town" continued to be sent and grasped.

Ana and I hosted a potluck dinner at our home to discuss how new members of our community and new students were being treated. I asked, "How should we teach about this in the schools?" Attending were Gorham teachers: Cheryl Wattsen, Zack Barber, Lacey Walsh, John Browne, Karla Betts, Jake Spanner, April Danniels, Charles Yates, and Angela Tremonte.

Angela commented first, "We should invite more immigrants into the United States and welcome them into Gorham. They enrich our country and become part of us."

"I agree with Angela. New arrivals are often escaping tyranny and persecution. I believe we should help them come into our country to live and prosper along and among us," Jake Spanner said.

"We need more workers in this country. Also, we should pay them a decent wage so they can support their families," Cheryl Wattsen said.

"You liberals will crowd us out of our own country. We have enough people in the United States and don't need any more," Charles Yates said. "Furthermore, immigrants go on welfare and never get off. We pay taxes to support them, and already pay too much in taxes, so this is the wrong cause to support. The immigrants are mostly low-income. Many are impoverished and go on our welfare system costing us valuable resources. Some have criminal records. We do not need additional criminality in this country. We have enough already."

"Charles, you threw the kitchen-sink into your argument with a litany of wrongs that immigrants allegedly commit. I believe the evidence indicates most immigrants are more law-abiding than many United States citizens and make significant contributions to our society," John Browne said.

"It is America first, Cheryl, John, and the rest of you.

Americans should come first," Charles responded.

"How about being humane to other people, Charles? Isn't that the American way?" Cheryl asked.

"No, Cheryl, it isn't the American way," Charles answered. "Throughout our history, the United States Congress has passed legislation controlling immigration. The 1920s experienced a significant push to control who could come into this country. There were efforts both before and after 1924 when President Calvin Coolidge, a former governor of Massachusetts, signed a stringent immigration bill into law," Charles said.

"Charles, is this the kind of nation we want to be—an anti-immigrant nation?" Cheryl asked.

"Oh, Cheryl, once again, you liberals are going overboard," Charles said.

"Charles, I believe the United States should open our borders—not close them off to eligible immigrants," Cheryl said.

Chapter 16: Hate

"What did they do?" I asked.

"Several Bailey High students saluted each other in the school building," A breathless Jake Spanner said after running up to me on Monday morning of a new school week.

"Why is that a problem?" I asked.

"The salutes were accompanied by 'Heil Hitler.' They were Nazi salutes."

"Ouch! Are you sure, Jake? Where did you hear this?" I asked.

"I heard about it this morning when I picked up coffee in the Town Square Coffee Shoppe. Several members of the public are outraged students would use the salute in their town's high school. There are retirees in town who fought in military battles themselves or had relatives in World War II fighting against the Nazis. Gorham's townsfolk are planning to take the issue to the School Board," Jake said.

"If the incident did happen as reported, we need to decide what to do. And, if these students did what is claimed, Jake, what possessed the students to do it?" I asked.

"Well, I talked with faculty before school this morning.

They thought it may emanate from the play the school's theatrical group—*Gorham Acts*—is working on. The play is about the White Rose group which was a youth group active in countering the Nazis in Germany prior to World War II. The salute is used in the play," Jake said.

"I have heard about the White Rose movement activism in Germany before the second World War," I said. "In context, the salute in a play may be permissible. The problem then, Jake, is if the students are saluting each other in school outside of play rehearsals. I wonder if members of the public are protesting the use of the salute in the play in addition to objecting to the saluting elsewhere in the school?"

"Apparently, the protestors have heard about the salute, and they don't care about the context. They are about to make noise and go to the school board about the saluting. The malcontents are also writing letters to Gorham's newspaper, the *Gorham Daily News*," Jake said.

"Potentially, Jake, the critics will be after any teacher who would have 'allowed such a thing' in Bailey High," I said.

"This is getting way out of hand. The White Rose faction defied Nazism. If it is clear in the play that the salute is in the context of opposing the Nazis, then there should not be a problem," Jake said.

"I don't think the activity in the play is the difficulty. The quandary is the fact that the salute has been used in Bailey High School hallways, and maybe outside the school building," I said. "We need to discuss this in class. In fact, we should have anticipated this might happen."

"I agree we should face the issue of the Nazi salute straight-on. However, I believe we ought not stop there," Jake said.

"What are you thinking of Jake?"

"Mark, the symbols of hate are all around us. We all know what has happened to some immigrant families here in town. Also, I conducted research about hate groups throughout our nation. Some of them are fiercely anti-immigrant like what we have seen manifested in Gorham," Jake said.

"Jake, what did you discover in your research?" I asked.

"Well, there are websites claiming there are over a thousand hate groups in the United States," Jake said.

"Holy Mackerel, I had no idea there was that much hate out there in our country and so many groups promoting hatred," I responded.

"Mark, your favorite saying is 'Holy Mackerel' when you are shocked," Jake said with feigned surprise.

"Yes, indeed, I am shocked. One thousand hate groups mushrooming into each other, and an 'America First' movement—that is hard to believe. We saw a similar movement prior to World War II," I said.

"There is more to be concerned with," Jake said.

"I am listening. What else could there be?" I asked.

"Some of the hate groups are targeting immigrant families like those who have moved to Gorham recently. Along with the salutes to Nazis, there is a wave of prejudice in town against anyone who is different. The immigrants have already suffered enough and are not being accepted as citizens in Gorham," Jake stated. "The America firsters mean implicitly—Nordic only."

"Damn it. This is the eugenicist's dream all over. Where does all this hatred stop?" I asked not expecting an answer.

"That I don't know. What I have said so far identifies only part of the problem in our larger society. In addition to the hatred of those who are 'not American enough,' there is the violence directed to those who do not stand for the singing of the 'Star-Spangled Banner' or for the 'Pledge of Allegiance,'" Jake said.

"Americans died for that flag," I stated. "So, I don't believe people should be compelled to stand and salute. Autocratic regimes require such obedience. Societies calling themselves democratic do not command saluting. In a free nation, citizens can salute or not as they see fit."

"Mark, 'the must stand and salute' advocates make the same argument you just did. They too say, 'We died for the flag.' Their position is expressed loudly and clearly. Proponents of their form of patriotism say to those who remain seated—'either stand, or else.'"

"Where is all this going, Jake?" I asked.

"I don't know, but as a community and country we are going down a slippery slope into a difficult to get out of rabbit hole," Jake responded.

After I received reports some of my students had been observed saluting "white power," I realized I had to discuss the issue in class. I asked my students, "Why do you think there is hatred in the world?"

"Mr. M., it is clear to me that there are some bad people in the world," Jody said.

"Jody, when you say, 'bad people,' who are you talking about?"

"That one is easy for me to answer, M. M., you know, bad people like killers, robbers, and so forth," Jody responded.

"If people use the Nazi salute, would you call them 'bad' people?" I asked.

"Not necessarily. All they do is salute. What is the problem with that?" Jody challenged.

"Bobbi, you wanted to comment," I said.

"Yah, Mr. M., there is a lot wrong with making the

Nazi salute," Bobbi said.

"What are you thinking of, Bobbi?" I asked.

"Well, the Nazi salute is offensive to a lot of people, and it is offensive to me," Bobbi said.

"Oh, come on Bobbi, it is just a salute. It doesn't mean anything," Jody responded.

"Oh, yes it does, Jody. It is symbolic of hate," Bobbi said.

"Would anyone else like to say something about any of the issues we are discussing?" I asked.

"Yes, Mr. M., I would," Albert said.

"Go ahead, Albert," I said.

"I hear what Bobbi is saying. However, back to the question of immigrants, I am not against all immigrants, just some immigrants," Albert said.

"I agree with Albert. There are some immigrants who should never have been let into this country, and some we should send back to where they came from. Like Albert said, not every immigrant—but some," Zeke said.

"How do you make that determination, Zeke?" Marta asked.

"I think it is obvious," Zeke responded.

"I don't agree, Zeke—it is not obvious!" Marta said.

"We can't settle this right now because our time in class today is coming to an end. Maybe Zeke and Marta can continue the discussion outside of class and report what you come up with," I said.

"I am game if Marta is," Zeke said.

"I am game, Zeke, so let's go for it," Marta said.

"It is a good idea, Marta, Zeke and everyone, to civilly discuss issues outside of class. Doing so extends our learning," I said.

"Mr. M., have you heard about some students organizing a White Student Union?" Aaron asked.

"What are they doing?" I asked incredulous.

"Yah. They are. The reasoning is that the school should be for a White Student Union because we already have a Black Student Union. So, why not a white one?" Diane asked.

"A White Student Union is just a cover for white supremacy. We all know that," Denni said.

"Then why do we have a Black Student Union?" Troy asked.

Chapter 17: Marathon

"Were any of your students at the run?" Ana asked me.

There were over twenty thousand runners in the two thousand and thirteen Boston Marathon. On April 15, at 2:49pm, two bombs detonated near the finish line where crowds had assembled.

The explosion in Boston led the newscasts. In past years, some of Bailey High's students attended activities surrounding the Boston Marathon, and several of our students habitually take a day off from school to go into the city for the event.

Faculty are required to record students absent when they attend the race in Boston. Yet, when students travel the twenty miles from Gorham to the annual Marathon in the city, school administrators realize students have relatives and friends competing, or just want to witness the running of an historic race. Although unauthorized, most of Bailey's staff believe attending the Marathon even on a school day is a learning experience for the Bailey students who watch the run.

"Yes, Ana," I said. "Ben, who is in my class, and his cousin Josh, told me they planned to go to the Marathon. Upon hearing the news of the deadly blast in Boston,

I wanted to find out if our students are safe. I feared calling the students' families and frightening them more than they probably already were."

"So, what did you do?" Ana asked.

"I asked anyone who might know if Ben and Josh were at the Marathon when the explosion struck," I said.

"Were they?"

"Yes, Honey, they were. While waiting to hear about my students' well-being, I received a call from Josh's mother. She reported Josh had called informing her that he and Ben were bodily okay. She also said Ben and Josh were close to the injuries. Apparently, both students became physically sick from what they saw and experienced. No one should have to witness what those at the Marathon did," I said.

"Especially, two so young. How are they emotionally?" Ana asked.

"When the bombs erupted, Josh was in a coffee shop getting something to eat and drink. He witnessed the horror through the window. What he saw left Josh traumatized," I said.

"How about your other student, Ben—where was he and what was the impact on him?" Ana asked.

"Ben was on the sidewalk adjacent to the runners. When the bomb erupted, he met death for the first time," I responded. "I cannot imagine what Ben and Josh saw and felt."

After they returned from the Boston Marathon, Ben and Josh spent time at home before returning to school.

The double explosion killed three people and injured over two hundred and fifty. The numbers denote the physical injuries. For most of the event's participants—competitors and witnesses—the psychological and emotional consequences can be ever-lasting.

Neither Ben nor Josh has ever talked to anyone about that day.

Chapter 18: Trafficking

"Mark, we heard from Tamela's grandmother that Tamela and Cammie have not returned home," Jake Spanner said before school on Monday morning at the beginning of the school week.

"What? What happened, Jake?" I asked.

"Tamela's grandmother said both Bailey High students were staying for the weekend with a friend who attends a neighboring school. Tamela and Cammie were supposed to return home on Sunday evening to get ready for school, but neither of them has been seen or heard from since Saturday night," Jake said.

"What do you think is up, Jake? Is there any reason for concern?" I asked.

"I don't know what to think at this point. Tamela was supposed to be in my first period class—she never showed."

"Do you know anything else?" I asked.

"Just that Tamela lives with her grandmother. Apparently, it is unlike Tamela to take off without telling anyone, especially her grandmother," Jake said.

"How about Cammie?" I asked. "Jake, you said no one has heard from her either. Is that right?"

"Yes, that's right. I have Cammie in my second period

history class. She did not show for class either," Jake said.

"Any idea at all where she is?" I asked.

"Unfortunately, I have no information and hesitate to speculate where either Tamela or Cammie might be," Jake responded.

"Does the school's staff know anything at all?" I asked.

"No, Mark. On Monday morning, Bailey High administrators were unsuccessful in attempting to reach Cammie's guardian," Jake said.

"Any luck since then?" I asked.

"Yes, I did receive some information this morning. I am not sure how helpful it is. School counselor Albert Standwicke finally reached the guardian after she returned home from work around seven in the evening," Jake said.

"What did Mr. Standwicke find out?" Jake asked.

"Cammie's guardian, like Tamela's grandmother, reported to Albert that Tamela and Cammie were supposed to be back to their homes Sunday evening. When neither girl returned to get ready for school the next day, it was hoped the two girls might be with someone else, skipping school, or there may be another explanation for their absence," I said.

"I hope this is all explainable," Jake said.

"Me too. As the hours have gone by, Tamela's mother and Cammie's guardian are becoming ever more concerned about Tamela and Cammie, their safety, and whereabouts. I hope we find out what is happening soon," I said.

By Wednesday morning, three days after they were last seen, there was still no news about Cammie and Tamela. I and the rest of Bailey High's staff became more apprehensive.

At the end of school Wednesday afternoon, two Gorham police detectives arrived at Bailey High. One of the detectives informed school counselor Albert Standwicke, "We found a student from a nearby high school out on the highway walking toward her home. She told us that she and two other girls had been picked up by a man and a woman heading south. The student told us that she and the other girls, matching the descriptions of Cammie and Tamela, had been prevented from leaving the vehicle."

When I was able to meet with Mr. Standwicke, I asked him, "How did the other girl get away?"

"When the driver stopped for gasoline, the girl reported that she faked going to the rest room and took off when no one was looking. The police said that the girl informed the officers that the perpetrators were more interested in Cammie and Tamela because of what they look like," Albert said.

I called the history and social studies faculty together before the first school bell rang to start the next day. I stated what I knew, "Before our meeting this morning, the police notified me that the student who escaped from the car on Wednesday said to the officers she overheard the couple planning to use the girls as 'bait' to entice men. The perpetrators then intended to rob the men. That is all the girl who escaped the vehicle provided to the police. The officers had no further information."

After being taken, Cammie and Tamela have not returned home. The authorities have not received any reports regarding where the two Bailey T. S. Memorial High School students might be located.

Chapter 19: The Room

"What happens in there?" Andie asked. "It seems to be such a secretive place. We students never get to see what is going on when teachers are in the room. I snuck in after school one day when no one was there."

The Room has various monikers: "Teachers' Room," "Faculty Room," "Work Room," "Office Suite," "Faculty Lounge." In Bailey T. S. Memorial High School, the students have simply branded it, "The Room," a moniker more mystery than endearment.

Students, who for one reason or another need to go to the room, knock gently on the room's hardwood door. If there is no answer, they daringly knock more firmly. A staff member, if moved to do so, opens the door, and asks the student, "What do you want?" Generally, students get the point that they are disturbing a room meant exclusively for teachers and school staff.

I had spent some time in the room, but not much. I had either been too busy with preparation and working with students individually, or I did not want to partake in social chatter. Besides, Ana and I had our occasional Friday night potlucks with colleagues where we had time to discuss educational, social, and personal issues, so I didn't spend much time in the room.

Shortly after I joined the faculty in Memorial High, the detectable smoke and over-flowing ashtrays had vanished. Smokers stepped outside of Bailey's outer walls to inhale and to exhale. In inclement weather, smokers found overhead shelter. Administrators eventually nudged 'puffers' away.

Over the years, I have learned what went on in the room depended on the occupants. The inhabitants—occasionally engaging in banter, making copies for class, grading papers, and preparing instruction—set the agenda.

During a discussion over Saturday morning coffee, Ana asked me, "Mark, what occurs in 'The Room' in Bailey High?" Before I could answer, she continued, "Those of us who teach in elementary school have little time for socializing. Those of you who teach in the upper grades seem to have more time to congregate and shoot the breeze."

"I sense a bit of sarcasm mixed with envy, Honey, or maybe even a smidgen of disdain—or a healthy portion of each," I said.

"Very perceptive, Mark," Ana said smirking.

"Well, Ana, a little of everything transpires in 'The Room.' You used the word 'socializing.' That is only part of what goes on. When I sporadically spend time there, I and other teachers exchange rumors, talk about family, debate sporting events, and proffer vacation ideas. Lest you think any of this is frivolous, you may be surprised that we do have intellectual discussions now and then," I said.

"I would hope so," Ana said with a wry smile.

"And, as I said, Ana, when we are in the room some of us even work on class preparation and grading depending on the press of time and who is in there to converse with."

"That sounds productive, Mark. Yet, you are repeating yourself."

"Okay—whatever—at other times we chat, we rest, we joke, we snack, we drink coffee, and use the rest rooms. How am I doing, Honey? Do you need me to say more?"

"No, I get it," Ana assured me.

"Do you need more details?" I asked.

"Like I said, I get it, Honey."

Chapter 20: Anxious

Pressure unsettles my students. Their nerves fray when they take standardized exams. Faculty attempt to ease the stresses stacked on high-stakes examinations—to no avail. The nonverbal messages passed to our students are clear—the test scores matter—they matter a lot. The gravity of the test scores weighs on the test-takers, so much so that they come to believe their futures hang on a test score.

Parents and school administrators emphasize the tests' importance. Adults tell students they need a high score to advance their chances of getting into the "right" college. Students are told a good college education leads to high compensation and a fulfilling career.

School administrators alert test-takers their standardized test scores also reflect on the merits of their school and of their parents. As a result, student anxiety grows as every little thing becomes a big thing. The prospect that poor scores sabotage a young person's future is sung in chorus—the singsong shatters the innocent.

Parents press for high scores, especially when high scorers collect scholarships. Scores earning merit awards yield highly prized cocktail party congratulatory chatter.

Schools compound the longing for the coveted bragging rights. Publicity machines celebrate institutional success in acquiring high standardized test scores, exclaiming for all to hear, "Look how good we are."

The month of March in my daughter's sophomore year in high school found Suzie in bed most of the day. She remained there on school days.

After observing my students and Suzie's response to the stress resulting from the test-score craze, I decided to write an article for my alma mater's alumnae magazine.

"To the Editor:

"My name is Mark Blenchard. I am a high school teacher at Bailey T. S. Memorial High School in Gorham, Massachusetts. I graduated from the university in 1970.

"I have been teaching in Bailey High since my graduation. I am writing because over the years I have observed the multiple stresses placed upon my students. I believe the pressures negatively affect the students and their families.

"Demands on our high school students have grown as high stakes standardized testing has become more important to parents, schools, and students. After the No Child Left Behind law took effect in 2002, the pursuit of high scores accelerated—resulting in increased apprehension.

"Adding to the strain, admission to selective colleges and 'prestigious' state universities has become even more competitive. This leaves many deserving students seeking matriculation wherever they can.

"Evidence is clear that students from families with greater incomes obtain higher test scores than those without test-taking advantages. The employment of expensive tutors has intensified the effort to gain an edge over those who cannot afford the expense as well as for those who can. Families end up groveling for a number on a test.

"Furthermore, the No Child Left Behind legislation has led to the evaluation of teachers and administrators based on test scores. Salaries and job security have become dependent on how well students do on exams written by anonymous individuals who do not know the students. Consequently, the students intuit the tension. When test day approaches, we ask them how they are doing. Their answers reveal the panic. The test-takers believe their entire lives rest upon THE TEST.

"The pressure is overwhelming for some students—unnecessarily so. Around test time, teen angst permeates the school community. The cruel bromide, 'suck it up,' leaves little time for living in the present.

"If students do not have the money, the expensive test-reparation-game leaves them outside looking in. The more effective the test preparation industry is in gaming the system—then the more expensive it is for the students and the students' families who purchase the assistance. In addition, there generally is no free bus service to the test preparation classes so a car is necessary—further widening the family-income gap for the carless.

"Thus, those who do not have the money play the college admissions game at a disadvantage. Meanwhile, students who have the privilege go to selective colleges which anoint them with more privilege enabling them in gathering ever more privilege.

"I have written this to my alma mater for publication because I believe it is important for others to know what one high school teacher and graduate from this institution has witnessed.

"Thank you.
"Mark Blenchard"
The University declined to publish my letter.

Chapter 21: Warriors

In October of 2004, my students wanted to know why we were at war in Iraq for what seemed to them had been forever. The United States invaded Iraq in 1991, toppling their leader Saddam Hussein. Here we were years later still battling in Iraq.

I asked the students, "Why do you think we are in Iraq?"

"Mr. M. I don't know," Patty said. "I thought we were at war with them before when George H.W. Bush was president. So, why are we still at war with them—and now with George W. Bush as president? It is all so confusing and futile to me."

"Patty, in 2002, we began fighting in Iraq again. So, you are questioning why we still have troops in Iraq—is that what you are asking?"

"Yes, Mr. M., that is what I am asking. We defeated them once so why are we spending all this money and American lives to fight the Iraqis once more?" Patty asked.

"Jenny, you want to say something," I said.

"Mr. M., Iraq attacked us on September 11, 2001. That is why we went to war with them again and continue to be at war with them," Jenny contended.

Richard responded, "No, the Iraqis didn't attack us on 9/11. It wasn't them who attacked us."

"Then who did it?" Jenny asked.

"It was a group of terrorists," Richard said.

"I doubt it. I have always heard it was Iraq who attacked us. My uncle served in Iraq and told me that," Jenny said.

My students were trying to understand what the conflict with Iraq was about. They read and heard about American soldiers maimed and killed in Iraq. Some of these students could soon be involved in the combat, so their interest heightened because of the personal implications. They implored to know why they and their friends might die—they wanted to understand.

Andy asked, "Mr. M., what is going on, how did this war happen, and why are we still fighting?"

"Those are tough questions," I said.

I turned to the students and asked them, "We have all heard various motives for invading Iraq. What are some of them?"

"Mr. M., I think it is in fact tied to 9/11," Eileen said.

"How so, Eileen?" I asked.

"I agree with Jenny. The Iraqis attacked us before we invaded them. They started it. That is why we are at war with them, and we are going to finish it," Eileen said.

"No Iraq didn't start it. Vigilantes did," Richard repeated.

"How do you know?" Jenny asked.

"Because I have been paying attention," Richard said.

"I have too. You tend to play one-ups-man-ship, Richard, so don't make condescending statements suggesting some of the rest of us have not been paying attention," Jenny said. "I have also been reading about what has been happening."

"Yah, I have too. I have been comparing sources—one with another. We have learned to do that from M. M. and our other teachers. Isn't that what you have been teaching us—to compare sources?" Richard said.

"Richard, Jenny and everyone, yes, checking out multiple sources through multiple media gives us a chance to arrive at a fair representation of what is going on," I said. "Bonnie, you want to say something."

"Yes, I do. Mr. M., you have to admit it is a lot of work to come up with a conclusion about what is going on in the political world," Bonnie said.

"Yes, Bonnie, it is a lot of work checking and comparing more than one source. Discovering the truth is not easy. As we have discussed in class before, to have a chance of arriving at the truth..."

Before I could finish, Michael said, "Oh, Mr. M., we know what you are about to say—we need to study and examine multiple sources through multiple media."

"Yes, I was just about to say that again," I said as the students laughed.

"We get the point, Mr. M.," Karen said to more laughter. "We get the point."

"Alright, you have my number, but it is an important concept," I said. "Daniel, you have something you want to say."

"Why don't we just let someone we trust tell us what is going on?" Daniel asked. "That would save us a lot of work."

"Because then some other people would be controlling you and what you think. As citizens, we all have to think for ourselves," I responded.

"That is a lot of hard work," Albert said.

"Albert and everyone, I believe citizenship is worth it. And knowing what is going on in the world affects us all," I said.

"But, Mr. M., if something doesn't impact us directly, why should we know about events that have no immediate effect on us?" Albert asked.

"I beg to differ. Especially in the international situation we have been discussing. Whatever happens elsewhere in the world affects all of us as citizens of the United States," I said.

"Explain that to us, Mr. M. I believe we should be concerned with what is occurring here in the United States and in this time," Cindie said. "Why, Mr. M., are these international events relevant to us?"

"Well, using what is materializing in Iraq as an example, we have students in this class who have had and some still have relatives involved in the Iraq conflict. Also, some members of the Bailey High and Gorham communities may soon be in Iraq or serving in the military elsewhere in the world," I said. "Carol, you want to make a comment."

"I get what you are saying, Mr. M. What happens in the rest of the world affects us all—even here in the United States, and it affects some of us personally," Carol said. "My relatives are deeply interested in these issues. I believe we should keep talking and learning about these events, then we would understand more. As a result, we would be better prepared to talk about and vote on these important issues. Going to war against others affects us all in this class, our families, and the rest of the country."

"Mr. M., in addition, we have a presidential election coming up, and we still have troops in Iraq. We need to keep talking about what is happening in the world so we will know what to do as citizens," Mamie said.

"What do any of you think the outcome of the election should be? Also, what do you think it will be?" I asked.

"I don't have an answer for that, Mr. M. How can I

have an impact on the election? I cannot vote yet. In a couple of months my brother is supposed to be coming home from Iraq. I do not want him killed or wounded for a cause I do not believe in. I wish I could vote, but I am not old enough. I hope whoever is elected will bring my brother home. So, I don't care who is elected as long as Rob is brought home to our family," Ricardo said.

"My cousin, Paul, is a nurse in the army. Will he be in danger if he goes to Iraq?" Jenny asked.

"Yah, he could be. I hear of IED's all over the country killing and injuring G.I.'s. Isn't that right Mr. M.?" Jimmy asked.

"Yes, Jimmy, but that does not mean that will happen to Jenny's cousin or Ricardo's brother. What do some of the rest of you think?" I asked.

"I think we are going to be there for a long time, and it is going to cost a lot in money and lives," Issac said.

"It is the loss of relatives for some of us in this class, and possibly my relatives, that really gets to me," Aisha said. "I, too, have a cousin in Iraq. I want to see her come home safe and sound," Aisha said.

"So, Aisha, what do you believe our position on Iraq should be?" I asked.

"We need to get out of there as soon as we can. What happens in Iraq does not affect us," Aisha said.

"Aisha, should we just let the terrorists take over. Is that what you want?" Donald asked.

"Of course I don't want that," Aisha said.

"What do you or others in this class want in this world of ours?" Bobby asked.

"I want peace which begs the question: Why do we keep getting involved in these military conflicts?" Sarah asked.

"Because we have to," Ben said.

"I wish we could vote. Why can't we, Mr. M.?" Eddy

asked.

"If we could vote, I would vote for America first. We should keep to our own business," Sarah said.

"We get into these conflicts. American soldiers die. We continue involving ourselves in military interventions—one after another. What are we doing getting into all these international predicaments?" Maria asked.

"Yah, Mr. M., what progress are we making in all these conflicts—if any?" Marco added.

"Is our national self-interest at stake?" Bettina asked.

"Is it?" I asked.

"No, I don't believe it is," Ned said.

"I agree," Bettina said. "It isn't in the interest of the United States to be entangled in all these battles around the world."

"If we stayed out of other people's disputes, we wouldn't keep getting in these messes," Jenny said.

"I disagree with what Jenny stated," Elbert said. "If we stayed out of international conflicts, I think it would be worse. Those who want to do us harm and hurt our way of life would be coming after us over here in the U.S., like what happened on December 7, 1941, when Japan attacked us at Pearl Harbor in Hawaii."

"Should we be in isolation as we were before World War II, and let the rest of the world fend for itself?" I asked.

"No, Mr. M., that is a loaded question you just asked us. However, I will answer it—of course not. We definitely need to be involved in the world," Alan said.

"The bell is about to ring. As always when we get into these seemingly intractable problems, we all need to keep thinking. Also, as citizens we have to stay current on what is happening in the world and reflect upon events occurring in other countries that are affecting the United States," I said.

"Hey, Mr. M., you and members of this class keep leaving us with more issues and questions than we have answers," Norma said as she was walking out of the room.

"Norma, do you think that is a good thing," I said.

"It probably is, but it is frustrating," Norma said.

"Maybe we just have to think ourselves through the frustration," I said.

Norma sighed as she said while walking out of class, "Like I said, Mr. M., that is frustrating."

Chapter 22: Clara

"Hi Mark. Why don't you and Ana come down to visit me in Appalachia. Maybe you could take the trip in late June when there is a break from teaching school. The weather is good here at that time of year, so it would be a great time to see the blooming vegetation, explore the parks, and visit.

"We could also go to Gatlinburg, window shop, walk the trails, check out historic sites, talk about our lives, and eat some great food. A drive through the Great Smoky Mountains National Park with lunch along the way would be great fun. We might even see a bear or two. What do you think?"

Claudia Pace's email to us arrived at the right time. Ana and I were completing a busy year of teaching, so the idea of traveling to and through the Appalachians and breathing fresh mountain air sounded delightful to us. Besides, we wanted to hear what life has been like for Claudia since she left Bailey T. S. Memorial High School to return to what she called "home."

In my response, I wrote, "Hi Claudia, your proposal sounds great. Ana and I need a break after a busy school year. We have read and heard about the beauty of Appalachia, but we have never been there. We would love to explore the area with you.

"If it works for you, we can plan to drive from Gorham shortly after we take care of things here. We should be in your area by the last full week of June when the flora should be at its height. Thank you very much for the invitation. Best wishes, Mark."

Ana and I arranged to meet Claudia in a centrally located cafe near where she lived. Though it had been a while since we taught together in Bailey High, we recognized her as soon as she walked into the appointed coffee shop. "Hi Claudia. You look the same as when we last saw you," I said.

"Thanks, Mark, and hello Ana," Claudia said.

"You are welcome," I responded.

"I guess, Mark, it is a good thing that I look much the same so you could find me. It has been more than a few years now since we last saw each other," Claudia said.

"Yes, it has been a while," I said.

"However, Mark and Ana, if you look closer you will see I have found ways to cover the graying process and the sprouting white hair," Claudia said. "You can judge for yourself if I have been successful. Anyway, I am thinking of letting it all grow out as nature takes its course. I am getting older, or should I say, more mature—might as well show it."

"I can't see the white, or even the gray. I would have to look a lot closer," I said with a laugh. "Your face does seem to have more color than it had when you were in the northeast."

"I have spent a lot more time in the sun here in Appalachia, so I have a year round tan. In New England, the tanning season is shorter," Claudia said smiling. "So, yes, you probably do see some physical changes—although, I trust not radical ones. On the other hand, my mental outlook has undergone more change.

"Ana and Mark, I have been doing all the talking. How are the two of you doing?" Claudia asked.

"Before we tell you about our lives, you just said something about your 'mental outlook.' I want to come back to that," I said.

"Claudia, you asked about our lives. We are busy with teaching—trying to do the best job we can," Ana said.

"Knowing the two of you, I am sure you continue to be exemplary educators," Claudia said.

"Thanks. I hope you are right about that," Ana said.

"I am convinced I am," Claudia responded.

"In addition, Claudia, both of our children, Joel and Suzie, are off living their lives now—so, we are empty-nesting," I said. "I hope we aren't interfering with your work and life by visiting here for a week. Any time you can spend with us, we would value."

"You are not interfering at all. I love having you and Ana here for a visit. I am all yours, at least, as much of me as you want and can handle," Claudia said.

"Claudia, you said something about your mental outlook which suggests some changes in how your life and work are going. I hope you are okay in that regard. If you are willing to tell us, what has life been like for you since we last saw you?" Ana asked.

"Well, that requires an explanation. First, however, please bring me up to date on what has occurred in your lives and in Gorham, Massachusetts, then I would be glad to fill you in on me."

"Claudia, you are avoiding or at least delaying talking about yourself," I said frowning at her evasion. "We will have to get back to you. However, in response to your question, I would say Ana and I have been teaching as well as we are able within the parameters we are contained. Other than our children, teaching is the center of our lives."

"Mark, you mentioned the parameters in Gorham. I am assuming you are talking about the political structure. Has the town of Gorham as a community changed politically? Also, has its school system become more progressive at all since I left?" Claudia asked.

"Well, Claudia, as I am sure you recall when you were in Gorham, it was not a very open-minded place and still isn't. So, not much has changed. The town has customarily resisted change and continues to do so—tradition governs," I said.

"Mark, it sounds like the place I was in before I moved down here. I remember the 'keep things the way things have always been' ethos that prevailed in Gorham when I was there. I remember it well."

"The same conservative doctrine governs today, Claudia, so you would still recognize the community and the locals' restricted—and some would say—constricted view of life," I said.

"You would think that in a so-called liberal state like Massachusetts, Gorham would be more hospitable to change, and would have changed over the years," Claudia said.

"Yes, Claudia, you would think the town would change. However, Gorham's governors work daily to keep things conventional and fixed in place. It may be a myth that the northeastern states and Massachusetts are all that liberal. Most locales in New England have long histories, and many towns with deep roots are insular, set in their ways, and aren't about to change old habits or customs," I said.

"Your comments beg the question: How are the schools doing up there in New England, and specifically in Gorham?" Claudia asked.

"As teachers in Gorham, we try to keep the schools

moving forward. By and large, I think we have been able to do some of that. At least, as much as we can in a community bound by and to its customs," Ana said.

"The 'moving forward' sounds positive," Claudia said.

"In part, we do move forward. In addition to Gorham's resistance to anything resembling change, national and state mandates affect what we do in the classroom. Federal mandates limit our ability to move in a progressive direction as far and as fast as we would like," I said.

"What dictates are you thinking of?" Claudia asked.

"Well, Claudia, as with the rest of the country, we give way too many standardized tests. From what I can observe in Bailey High and what I have witnessed with Joel and Suzie attending schools in Gorham, students take an excess of required examinations. I don't think the rest of Massachusetts is any different, or for that matter—states elsewhere in the rest of the country," I said.

"Ana, has the testing mania affected your younger students also?" Claudia asked.

"Unfortunately, Claudia, yes it has. My elementary school students are way over-tested. As a result of the test-mania, the children are permitted less playing time. They lack the opportunity and time to play, create and explore. We are always getting them ready for this test or that test," Ana said.

"Ugh—playing is what the younger students should be doing," Claudia said.

"I absolutely agree. The obsession with testing does not make sense to those of us who are teaching in the classroom every day," Ana explained. "The advent of the testocracy only makes sense to the politicians who have never been in classrooms as educators, but the policymakers think they know what is best for our students—they don't."

"Ana and Mark, I am sorry to say, it isn't any different here in Appalachia," Claudia said.

"Could you please explain?" I asked.

"Sure. In addition to the maze of tests showing many of our students scoring lower on the average than students in some parts of the rest of the country, we also suffer from an image problem."

"I need more information to understand what you mean," Ana said.

"The faulty imaging of who we are is used as a spurious justification for exploiting our resources," Claudia said.

"How does that work?" I asked.

"Well, Ana and Mark, we are called 'Hillbillies,' which has a negative connotation for some people. However, as I have said before, the young people in Appalachia are as smart as students anywhere else. We just show it in a different way—not on the standardized tests written by someone not from here who doesn't understand or know much about the young people who live here."

"How so, Claudia?" I asked.

"Well, Mark, many of my students here in Appalachia are pragmatic, conceptual thinkers who use ideas they believe will work as they confront daily challenges. These learners are hard workers and apply their knowledge. They wisely use what they learn to try to make the lives of people around them better. Generally, this kind of knowledge does not show up on STANDARDIZED exams," Claudia said.

"Claudia, I have not worked here in Appalachia, but what you just said makes sense to me. My elementary school students are like those you have described. The test-makers know little about my students. The testocrats have scant insight into what the test-takers know and can do. We should be emphasizing critical and creative thought rather than the standardized status quo thinking the exams measure," Ana said.

"Ana, what you say makes sense. Furthermore, exploiters of our resources feed off us because they believe 'those people' do not know any better. We do—we do know better. The standardizers tamp down learners who are different. I, my students, and their parents, are sick and tired of being exploited!" Claudia exclaimed.

"What you are saying, Claudia, rings true in my life and teaching experiences," Ana said.

"We have a lot of work to do where I teach now. And as you have said, in Gorham, Massachusetts—you do too. We should be teaching critical thinking and encouraging students to challenge the system, which is the last thing the people in power want us to do—question their legitimacy and entitlement," Claudia said.

"Yes, indeed, we have some work to do. The good news though is, and I think Ana will agree, we both work in Gorham with some energetic and committed colleagues. The educators I work with back home keep us sane and find ways through the system. We try to keep our eyes on the task—helping the students learn to question what is not working rather than to accept the way things have always been done," I said.

"Now, Claudia, it is your turn. How about you? What is happening in your life?" Ana asked.

"You two have made some important points. I have already mentioned some of what I have encountered in Appalachia. In addition, I have been involved in organizing educators to fight for our rights. Before I left Gorham in June of 1999, I said to Mark what I intended to do upon my return to Appalachia."

"What did you say to Mark at that time?" Ana asked.

"I told your husband I intended to assist the people in

Appalachia in any way I can," Claudia said.

"I remember what you said. I was and still am impressed with your commitment to help the students in the place you call home," I said.

"Well, Mark, I am sure you will not be surprised to hear it is still difficult getting organized. There are a lot of economic and societal forces fighting against teachers speaking for themselves and using their rights as educators and citizens. I have come nowhere near to organizing educators as I thought I could. It has been frustrating because of the built-in power structure, but I am continuing to do whatever it is I can," Claudia said.

"I understand the frustration in dealing with the established powers. It is something that continues to vex me and Ana too. So, Claudia, how about what is happening in your own classroom? What is that like?" I asked.

"As far as teaching goes, as in Gorham, I work with some outstanding teachers. The parents in this community are behind their children, and the students are great," Claudia said.

"Your description of those you are working with sounds like you are with some of the right people to educate students," I said.

"Yes, I believe I am. However, Mark, as in Bailey High and in Gorham, Massachusetts, there are a lot of people in my community who want to keep things the way they have always been. Also, I must say, there are formidable forces who want to keep young people under-educated. Under-educating young people in the community generates a source of cheap labor. The last thing some of the town fathers and mothers want us to do is help the students learn how to think critically, because then the thoughtful employees would not work for pennies in unsafe conditions."

"How do you bring about change then, Claudia?" I asked.

"The same way, I think, you do anywhere," Claudia responded.

"How's that?"

"One student at a time."

"By the way, Claudia, speaking about one student at a time, have you seen the student you told me about when you were teaching in Appalachia before you came to Gorham?" I asked. "I can't recall her name."

"I remember. Her name is Clara. I have not seen her since my return to Appalachia. Until recently, I had no idea how to reach her."

"You said, 'until recently.' What have you found out?" I asked.

"I had been inquiring about Clara for a while. Then I met a former student while shopping in the food market in town who knew something about her. What I heard was disturbing."

"What was that?"

"The student said she had not seen Clara after she dropped out of school. However, she did say she had heard about Clara," Claudia recounted.

"Go on, please," I urged.

"The student started by telling me that 'in the hills pain killers are easy to get.' She then said, 'I have heard Clara has taken more than her share.' I also learned that Clara lives in a trailer and supports herself selling anything she can, including herself. I then asked if we could find Clara, and maybe talk with her. The former student said she thought it might be arranged."

"Claudia, it might be worth trying to find and help Clara. This sounds dreadful," I said.

"If Clara needs and wants help, maybe we could help her," Ana said.

"I am not sure where Clara lives, but I will try to find out and see if she is willing to meet with us," Claudia said.

Claudia, Clara's former teacher, asked another student Claudia had in class when teaching in Appalachia where Clara could be found. In this case, the student was able to provide Clara's address and telephone number. Claudia called Clara and asked if she could visit, and if Ana and I could accompany Claudia. Clara consented, but said we could only meet with her "outside her trailer."

"Do you know why she wants us to meet outside the trailer?" I asked.

"I don't know why, but that is one of her conditions in order for her to talk with us," Claudia said.

We called ahead and met Clara outside her trailer. After cursory introductions, Claudia asked Clara, "How are you?"

"Alright, I guess," Clara said.

"Clara, how are you really doing?" Claudia asked.

"I'm doin' okay. Why do you keep asking?" Clara responded.

"I have heard you are not doing all that well," Claudia said.

"What exactly have you heard Ms. C., and who told you that shit?" Clara asked.

"Okay, Clara, I will cut to the chase. I have heard that you are using drugs and paying for your habit through selling your body," Claudia said as fast as she could say it.

"What's it to you, and I would like to know who the bastard or bitch is who fucking told you about me?" Clara asked.

"Well, I care about you. That is why I have asked about how you are doing," Claudia said.

"Oh, come on. You do-gooders all say that crap. I bet you told your friends you were coming back to the hills to help me and others like me. Well, Ms. C., I do not need your fuckin' help," Clara cried.

"Clara, you are a student of mine and always will be. I love all my students—every student is important to me. I care about you deeply."

"SERIOUSLY, you love all of us—me included. I do not believe it. If you really knew me, you would realize I am not lovable. I am a royal fuck-up," Tears reddened Clara's face.

"Clara, my friends and I are here to help you," Claudia said.

"Ms. C., I don't want to talk no more—I just want you and your friends to get out of my fuckin' face and fuck-off. I don't need your fucking help or anyone else's, so please, please—go away!"

Chapter 23: Jeff

Shortly after Ana, Claudia Pace, and I met with Clara, Claudia delivered the news, "Clara died from an overdose."

The stunning news shook, and shocked us, but, sadly, did not surprise us. We felt the desperation when we talked with Clara but had no helpful response.

We agreed to meet, took a long walk, and shed tears as we talked about the loss of Claudia's student.

We sat in silence in a local bakery until we could speak. We tried to determine what we should have done—maybe we should not have gone to see Clara.

In addition to talking about Clara, we asked Claudia about the assistant principal, Jeff Krizer, she had worked with in Appalachia when she taught there. Claudia said, "Clara had been coerced into falsely accusing her assistant principal of touching her in his high school office. The school system fired Jeff shortly thereafter."

"What happened with Jeff after that?" I asked.

"As a result of Clara's compelled, false accusation resulting in Jeff's removal as assistant principal, he decided to leave education as a profession," Claudia said. "In my view, Jeff leaving education is a big loss for students in Appalachia."

"What did Jeff do after he was let go as an assistant principal? He had to find work, didn't he?" Ana asked.

"Yes, he did need a job. So, after Jeff was summarily dismissed as an assistant principal, he married a woman who had two small children. She lived in a rural village about twenty miles from the school both he and I were employed in."

"So, Claudia, after being fired from his job, what has Jeff done to make a living?" I asked.

"Well, even though most of the fair-minded people in the educational community accepted his side of the story, Jeff realized it was unlikely he could get a job in education again because his name and the accusation were on the Internet—available for anyone with a computer connection to spot. As a result, education as a profession was out for him at least in the foreseeable future and maybe forever. However, Jeff is a talented guy."

"Talent helps, of course, but what could he do to pay the bills?" Ana asked.

"Ana, indeed, he did have to earn money for his family. He is handy with tools, so he has been able to make a living. Jeff can build almost anything," Claudia said.

"Claudia, have the accusations of impropriety with Clara harmed him in his new business?" I asked.

"No. The fabricated charges could not derail him because he works for himself and is competent. In addition, Jeff and his wife live a sustainable lifestyle. The couple grow their own food in a community garden. This has kept costs down, so he has maintained a quality life even though he is deprived his first love—educating young people," Claudia said.

"He probably misses teaching. Do you know if he

does?" I asked.

"He hasn't said those words, but I believe he does. In fact, knowing him the way I do, I am sure he does," Claudia said.

"It sounds like his personal reputation is intact for the most part. Is it?" Ana asked.

"Yes, he is well regarded. In his construction work, people who know him have given him the benefit of the doubt."

"Has he ever tried to get back into education?" I asked.

"Not to my knowledge. The fact Jeff is no longer an educator is a big loss for the citizens and their children who live here," Claudia stated. "He was a good educator when I worked with him. He would most likely be even better now that he has had work experience in another profession. If he were still in a school system, Jeff could share what he has learned in the work-world which is where many students will be entering. Regrettably, our schools have lost an outstanding mentor because of an unsubstantiated allegation."

"Claudia, although I did not know him, it sounds like the school he was in and the students of Appalachia have lost an educator in the true sense of the word," I said.

"Mark, I believe shoving Jeff out of education based on unfounded accusations is a travesty," Claudia said.

"Is there any hope he might get back into education?" I asked.

"I don't think so. Jeff has refused all speaking engagements or participating in conferences to discuss his experiences in education. He has also declined invitations to speak publicly about his work as a contractor building things. Losing Jeff's voice as an educator and citizen is a big loss—a big loss indeed."

"So, in addition to Jeff being out of the classroom, we will miss hearing the views of an outstanding educator. What a shame," Ana said.

"Yes, tragically, we no longer have Jeff as a practicing educator. However, he has written a short but important piece," Claudia said.

"He has composed something others can read?! Where can I find it?" I asked.

"He has written a short set of statements regarding his education philosophy. Therefore, Mark and Ana, we have not lost everything. I think you will find what he wrote interesting and significant."

"What did he communicate and has he spoken in public about his beliefs?" I asked.

"No, Jeff has not gone public. He is letting his written words speak for him. His composition is indicative of what kind of an educator Jeff has been, and the community participant he is," Claudia said.

"Do you have a copy of his statements?" I asked.

"Yes, I do. He has circulated his writing to a small group of friends and former colleagues. Would you and Ana like to read it?"

"Yes, of course—of course!" Ana nodded her head.

"I have copies at home. I will check with Jeff to see if he minds if I give the essay to those he does not know."

After Claudia received Jeff's consent, he provided us with copies of his education philosophy.

Ana and I separately read what Jeff wrote.

"Jeff Krizer's philosophy of education:

I have written the following for my children and for anyone else who is interested.

Here it is:

"This I believe—

All children are different from each other. As a result,

learners develop their personal education paths.

Teachers should assist students in reaching their full potential and in meeting their respective goals.

Educators need to identify a child's style of learning, adapt curricula to the child's unique mode of learning, and help students in expanding their individual learning patterns.

Once a child's interest is aroused, the teacher should help the child pursue that interest.

If we help children soar, they will go to places neither their teachers nor anyone else could have imagined."

After reading Jeff's philosophy, Ana said, "You know, Mark, in just five statements, Jeff says a lot."

"Yes, Ana, I agree. For me, and from what I learned from Ken Lewiston, Jeff's essay conveys the essence of educating," I said.

"It does, Mark. It certainly does," Ana said.

"Yet, we have lost him in the classroom," I said.

Chapter 24: Saturdays

In thinking about retiring, I wondered what I would do with my time. When a friend of mine said he had been attending a Saturday morning discussion group, I asked, "Burnie, what do you talk about in the discussions?"

"Anything that comes up. Mark, I think you would enjoy the give and take. Although we generally have a previously announced topic for discussion, the group spends some time on a current event if there is an important topic emerging in the news," Burnie said.

"Sounds like a classroom for retirees," I said with an amused smile.

"It is. Although, we have a few participants join us who are still gainfully employed and not fully retired yet. In the sessions, we discuss a variety of topics. Most of the issues are controversial. Unlike schools and universities, there are no tests and grades," Burnie said chuckling.

"If the issues are often controversial, do the discussions become heated?" I asked.

"Not really. Although we normally discuss contentious issues, the group handles any disagreements civilly—at least, for the most part," Burnie said with a sly smile.

"Sounds interesting. You said civility prevails 'for the most part,' so Burnie, when the group encounters dissension, do people leave with hard feelings?" I asked.

"No, I don't believe we do. There seems to be an implicit agreement that when we adjourn, we leave conflicts in the room. We wait until we meet again to go back at it. In general, the group is congenial and most of the participants keep coming back which is a sign of something," Burnie said grinning.

"That is impressive considering lots of political discussions dissolve into hard feelings. In some cases, people stop talking with each other after intense exchanges," I said.

"Yah, Mark, I understand that happens in some groups, but this is not a concern with the people meeting on Saturdays. We are mostly a friendly crowd. We keep any discord in the room and out of communal view," Burnie said with a wry laugh.

"That is commendable, and I must say—somewhat unusual."

"So, Mark, it sounds to me you are interested. Why don't you come with me next Saturday to see how the discussions go? As you contemplate retirement, you may find participating in the group is something you would like to do—maybe even on a regular basis," Burnie said.

"Burnie, you said the discussion meetings are called, 'Saturdays.' Do I have that right?"

"Yes, that is what we call the sessions. I realize it is not very original, but it is so-named because the sessions take place on Saturdays," Burnie said humored by my inquiry.

"Hmm. That makes sense—I guess," I said.

I decided to give the discussion group a try to see if it worked for me. Prior to accompanying Burnie to a Saturday morning session, he told me, "The sessions are held in the rear room of a restaurant. Most group members order coffee and a light breakfast. The discussions start at eight in the morning and slow down around 9:30am. After the sessions, group members mingle. Talking continues as participants exit the restaurant. Informal discussions frequently continue outside the café. Depending on the topic and interest in an issue, small groups continue conversing until lunchtime."

"Burnie, some prospective and actual retirees are on a tight budget. How much does each member contribute to rent space, and is there a membership requirement and dues?" I asked.

"Other than the cost of food and drinks, there is no charge for the meeting room. The dining and meeting areas are informal and without a smidgen of pretentiousness—our group fits right in.

"The owner and the staff appear to like having us around. There is no membership fee or requirement to purchase food or drink, so you can come and go without spending a dime. We generally leave a dollar or two on the table when we leave, but there is no requirement to do so," Burnie said.

"Is regular attendance necessary?" I asked.

"No, not at all. Individuals come and go. Most of the regulars attend frequently—no minimum number of times to join us is required. First names are used—no titles. We lack haughtiness. At least for the most part, informality prevails," Burnie said seemingly amused by his comment.

Burnie had convinced me, so I attended the next Saturday session. The announced topic stated as a question was, "Should the United States be involved in the affairs of other nations, or should we take care of ourselves and let other nations fend for themselves?"

The group's leadership rotates each Saturday. The discussion leader, identified as Jerri, led this session with the question regarding involvement in the affairs of other nations. She then opened the session for comments.

Joe, a military retiree, responded, "We should take care of ourselves. It should be America first and let other nations follow us if they want to. We should be answerable to our people and other countries should be responsive to their citizens. Each nation's self-interest should prevail in international affairs."

"I agree, Joe. We have enough problems here in this country without getting involved in other countries' quarrels," Margaret, a retired insurance agent, said. "Unless it directly affects us, we shouldn't worry about what other nations do. That is their concern, not ours. The first principle of any country is to further its own national welfare. Other nations need to be concerned with their own—we need to concentrate on ours."

Melissa, a recently retired postal employee, countered, "After World War I, the United States moved into isolation. That did not work out very well for the United States or the rest of the world—did it? Our isolated nation could not stay out of the next war engulfing the world."

"We still have not recovered from the last war with all the lives and material lost." Melissa continued, "So, we should be involved peacefully with other nations and assist them which will help the United States in the long-run. Therefore, I am a proponent of organizations like the Peace Corp and the United Nations."

"I disagree with you, Melissa," Manny, a retired teacher, said. "You sound like an internationalist. In my opinion, it should be America first, so I agree with Joe and Margaret. We should take care of the people of the United States first and let other countries fend for themselves."

"Sorry, Manny, we need to be involved in the world," Yvonne, a retired Gorham public works employee, said. "The stance you, Joe, and Margaret advocate is what got us into World War II. In the 1920's and 1930's, instead of being involved in world affairs, we made the mistake of staying out of the League of Nations. So, I agree with Melissa.

"In contemporary international affairs, withdrawing from involvement internationally is precisely the action that will lead to aggressive military excursions in the future. In my judgement, the 'America first' idea is a recipe for disaster and will lead us into unwanted and unnecessary wars," Yvonne concluded.

By the end of the Saturday session I attended, the internationalists and the nationalists broke roughly even in their declared positions. The group discussion ended without anything resembling an agreement. it was not chaotic—it was inconclusive. Open discussion led to this Saturday's open ending.

I found the first session intriguing enough to want to change an appointment I had scheduled, so I could make it to the next meeting. The Saturday group's subsequent topic was one I have spent my employment-life working on and in—education.

Burnie and I joined the gathering with the announced question, "What is the state of education in the United States today, and what changes should we, as citizens, propose?"

Caroline, who had taught third-graders for thirty years before retiring, began the discussion, "Our educational system is in shambles. We need to restore respect for teachers. I retired four years ago, and since that time I have seen our society increasingly disrespect educators. My colleagues are not paid what we should be, and we are frequently told what to do without consulting those who know what is best for students—classroom teachers. Some teachers cannot wait to retire because of the lack of respect. That is the way I see it. In my judgement, it is not the way it should be. Our society can't afford to lose effective teachers, especially when we are experiencing a teacher shortage."

"But, Caroline, our schools are not doing what they should be doing," Roberto, a retired construction worker, said.

"Roberto, what is it that you believe the schools should be doing?" Caroline asked.

"At the very least, students should learn how to read, write, count, and follow directions. Learning these skills, at a minimum, will help them get a job when they graduate," Roberto said.

"Roberto, how about learning about our government through civics courses? Also, young people should learn United States history, some world history, as well as herstory. Students are going to be citizens of the world and of the United States. Knowledge of herstory and history is necessary," Caroline said.

"I hear you, Caroline, but the educational system's primary job is to help young people learn a trade so they can get a job," James, still a part-time financial advisor, said. "Also, I want to come back to your comment on 'herstory.' I have heard that terminology before, but we should stay on one topic for now."

"I agree with James on everything he just said. Yes, our school graduates need to be good citizens—learn to obey laws and such—but first they also ought to learn how to make a living and support their families," Samuel, a retired medical technician, said.

"I disagree with James and Samuel. As Caroline

said, citizenship is the primary obligation of what the school should do. Employment is part of that, but just a part—not the primary reason for going to school," Barbara, a retired high school social studies teacher, said. "I also concur with Caroline that we should learn some herstory as well as history. Maybe we can even develop new terminology to describe our mutual pasts."

"Let me make sure I know what we are discussing," Warren said.

"What is school for is the question," Annea said.

"It is simple," John said. "

"What is so simple?" Annea asked.

"The answer is—a job—a job. Getting a job is why we go to school, and that is what we should be talking about," John said.

"I don't think that is the primary reason for getting an education," Barbara said.

"What is or should be the reason then?" My friend Burnie asked.

"Citizenship education—in short, to be good citizens," Anisha, a physician still practicing part-time, said.

"Anisha, can't you educate for both—a job and citizenship?" James asked.

"Yes, James, I agree that you can do both, but for me—educating citizens should be the main objective in school systems," Anisha responded.

"Maybe you can do both, Anisha, However, educating for employment should be the primary goal of schooling," Roberto asserted.

"Roberto, I don't agree with what you are saying or advocating," Barbara said as time ran out on this Saturday session.

After the meeting, Burnie and I talked about what we had experienced—heard and felt.

"What happens when the group's participants can't

or don't agree?" I asked Burnie.

"When the time is up, it just ends. People have other places to go. Most will be back the following Saturday."

"Even if there is no agreement?" I asked.

"Especially if there is no agreement. Most of us will return the following Saturday to see what happens next," Burnie said.

"If there is no agreement, then why do you keep doing it?" I asked.

"It is good to hear other views. It clarifies our own way of looking at things even if we don't change individual perspectives," Burnie said. "At our age, changing hard-won views is difficult to come by."

"What would you say the point of the discussion is if you and others don't change your views?" I asked. "Does it then just turn into a social occasion? If it does, what is the point if it is just to get together?"

"It is way more than socializing," Burnie said. "Even at a young age, it takes time to change views. It is even harder as we get older, but we have to keep going at it."

"So, your Saturday meetings are educational experiences—albeit the learning may occur over time. Do I have that right?" I asked.

"Yes, I think that explains it," Burnie responded. "It is an education for those of us who are a little older. However, Mark, I do have a significant concern when participating in this group."

"What is your concern?" I asked.

"Well, we generally have an equal number of men and women in the group—about thirteen men and thirteen women depending on the time of year. Yet, by a three to one ratio men talk more than women, and from my calculation men also talk longer when they do expound and propound. Furthermore, the men are louder and get even louder when they think they are not being heard."

"Ahh, that factor is interesting. So, Burnie, have you ever discussed the 'Me Too' issue during any Saturday session?" I asked.

"Yes, we have. It was discussed briefly, but it was so polemical the endeavor stopped shortly after it began," Burnie said. "It was the one subject we had to drop before we got very far into it."

Chapter 25: Reunion

I had not been to my high school class reunion since I graduated in 1966. Ana had another engagement, so she encouraged me to go alone.

When I returned home from the reunion, Ana asked, "How was the reunion, Mark?"

"How much time do you have, Ana?" I asked.

"Why did you ask that, Honey? You asked that question after you attended the conference about 1945, 1958 and 1968, and your explanation became a long narrative. Are you suggesting this also requires a protracted account?" Ana asked.

"Yes, this too is an engaging tale—although, maybe not as eventful as the conference about those years. However, I am willing to tell you about my class reunion if you are game for listening to the stories," I said.

"Honey, I always listen when you want to tell me something," Ana said.

"I realize you might be working me over. Anyway—here goes. This reunion report needs context. I believe it is a fascinating human chronicle of some importance. As I mentioned, it will take a while for me to tell the story," I said.

"I am enthralled. I really am. So, go for it. I am

listening."

"Alright. Ana, I am not sure every high school reunion has the personalities I am going to describe. Although, I wouldn't be surprised if what I encountered is what most people come across fifty years after high school graduation."

"Mark, this sounds like it will be intriguing and informative," Ana responded with an attentive smile.

"Yes, indeed, Ana, you are having a little fun with me; but I really do think there is some social and cultural relevance for us in analyzing high school reunions, and my experience in this one. It may broaden our thinking about what occurs after high school—but then it may not. In any event, I would like to tell you what occurred, and you can make of it what you will."

"I am paying attention. I really am. If it is significant to you, then it is to me."

"I get it."

"Go ahead then, Mark. I am all ears. What did you see and experience at your reunion?"

"Okay. First, and I hope you find this germane. I would think that every graduating class has a lover-boy who returns to the scene of conquest. You know, Ana, the guy who thought he was and still believes he is the gift that keeps on giving," I said.

"Hmmm. Keep going, Honey. By the way, Mark, were you the lover-boy?" Ana asked.

"No, I was not," I said.

"I believe you," Ana responded.

"Hmmm—oh, well—to continue: The 'lover' returning to his classmates has apparently convinced himself that he left broken-hearts behind after graduation. He walks and talks as if he were still seventeen and a high school senior. His reunion mission is to find and mend some of the hearts he broke, or at least repair them for the night. He may also believe that if he is lucky, he can break a heart or two again," I said.

"Yah, Mark, that does not sound like you. Tell me more. As you know, Mark, I never graduated from a public high school. I earned a G.E.D. in lieu of a traditional diploma. I missed the in-school involvement most teens have. I did not partake in the daily classroom interactions you did. I ran into lover-boys on the streets, not in the classroom. What you are saying makes sense, but I didn't live it the way you did."

"I am glad it does make sense. Therefore, I will continue," I said.

"Please do," Ana said.

"In addition, Ana, along with the self-appointed king of the prom, alias the lover-boy—there is the 'queen'—the object of male attention in high school. In the case of the reunion I attended, the queen has changed as has the king. The king was no longer the prized lover-boy. The queen, on the other hand, even though she too had added years, had retained her charm."

"I hear what you are saying, Honey. I wonder what my fellow students would say about me had I gone to a regular high school. As I hear you recount your reunion, it does make me contemplate what my classmates, if I had them, would have thought about me then compared to today and the changes decades have bequeathed."

"I have no idea what they would think about you. Maybe you lucked out and avoided the judgmental stares and the stereotyping."

"Maybe I did, and maybe I didn't. I have had my share of people scrutinizing me. For me, that was not and still is not a positive feeling. Maybe because of my lack of self-esteem, I suppose what they are thinking is not good."

"If they knew you, Ana, I believe the judgements

would be overwhelmingly positive."

"Maybe."

"They would. I am sure of it."

"As I said, Mark—maybe."

"Should I go on? There is more about my reunion."

"Yes, please do. I do see this conversation as important, and I believe it is revealing to both of us," Ana said.

"I agree," I said.

"So, Mark, please provide another example of a reunion returnee's fate," Ana urged.

"Okay, Ana. In my high school, there was the school nerd, which was a term occasionally used to describe me when I was in college. In high school, however, I was an athlete—the lingo used to describe me back then was—jock. Even when I became nerdy, I wasn't as nerdy as the guy in my high school I am about to describe."

"I think I get it. Go ahead, Mark. Once again, I am paying rapt attention," Ana said.

"Well, the nerd at my high school reunion no longer wore glasses. Science took care of that. It was also clear that the nerd had been distance running and chiseling his physique. Although he was along in years, he now looked like a well-conditioned high school jock."

"So much for the nerdy look, huh, Mark."

"Yah. Gone."

"So, Mark, was there someone there at the reunion who was actually the jock-type in your high school? I have heard about the jocks, and you said you were one in high school."

"Yes, I was, although I wasn't a genuine jock like the guy I could describe. Of course, if you want me to provide some details."

"Yes, indeed, Mark, please do. I am learning a lot about you as you describe others."

"That is interesting," I said.

"I am glad you hear it that way."

"Okay—to continue: My high school had more than one jock participating in different sports. Unlike the nerd, the guy at the reunion who was the football hero in high school clearly did not keep up his previous habit of lifting weights and working out. Honey, I am out of shape, but I am trying to stabilize my body-size. This former jock sat at my table washing down fat-laden food with bountiful swigs of beer adding girth to his already too large body while sitting in a chair way too small for his spacious frame. You get the picture don't you, Ana?"

"Yes, Mark, I do. I believe I do from your long descriptive sentence about this guy's post-high school physique. Are there more personages?"

"Oh, yah. many more, but I am going to concentrate on one story."

"This should be good."

"It is. In addition, I believe it is instructive and indicative."

"Indicative of? Once again, you have my attention."

"It will take a while."

"I am not going anywhere."

"Well, as is my practice at such crowded activities like the reunion, I sat at an inconspicuous table away from the middle of the room."

"Away from the action?" Ana asked.

"Yes, as far away as I could. At least, as far as I could perch without calling attention to myself."

"What happened next?"

"Well, Ana, sitting across from me was Delores Pratt, who was also apparently hiding out and trying to be invisible—which, as you will learn as I explain further, was a difficult task for her."

"Who is Ms. Pratt?"

"In the late 1960's, my high school group of friends were conformers—not protesters. Delores was part of the bound to tradition group. She was also the one everyone paid attention to—males because she attracted them and females because she attracted males."

"She sounds, I guess you could say—noteworthy. Did you talk with her?"

"Yes, I did."

"What did you say to each other?"

"I asked her, 'How are you doing Delores?'"

"Mark, that is inventive. What did she say to that?"

"Delores responded, 'Well, Mark, I am here.'"

"Then what did you say, Sweetheart?" Ana asked.

"I did not know what to say next, so I asked her, 'Between high school and being here today, what has happened in your life?'"

"'Mark, are you sure you want to know?' Delores responded."

"Did you want to know, Sweetheart?" Ana asked.

"Sure, and Ana, I remembered when April Danniels asked our potluck dinner group the same question. We received more information than we had expected. So, I said, 'Yes Delores, I would like to hear your story.'"

"Delores replied, 'I will begin this yarn by telling you that I have been married three times. I am in the process of my third divorce.'"

"'Oh,' I said."

"What else did she say?" Ana asked.

"She said, 'You know, Mark. I wish I had never been thought of as attractive.'"

"I responded to Delores, 'That is a strange comment coming from the class beauty.'"

"Delores then said, 'Mark, are you interested in an explanation as to why I said I didn't like to be thought of as an attraction?'"

"I said, 'Yes. Delores, I am interested.'"

"Delores then said, 'Well, I have come to know the scourge of being thought of as a beauty in this culture. This culture exploits the so-called beautiful and then spits them out when they are no longer of sexual utility.'"

"What did you say then, Mark?" Ana asked.

"I said to Delores, 'That is a strong statement containing words like, 'scourge' and 'exploit.' Your statement, however, is one I understand somewhat more now than I did in the past. Tell me more, Delores. I am intrigued.'"

"Delores responded, 'Well, Mark, when we were in high school, women were defined by what we looked like. We were playthings. Note, I did not use the terminology, 'girls.'"

"'Did the feminist movement help?' I asked. 'It was the latter part of the 1960's when you and I were in high school that the women's movement was gaining traction.'"

"Delores responded, 'No, it missed me and others like me. The feminist movement had little impact on the everyday lives of women. In fact, women are still treated as articles to be exchanged. We are objects—objectified, used, shunned when we age—then dispensed with. As I said, Mark, I am amid my third divorce.'"

"'The objectification statement is another strong one. Didn't feminism help at all in reducing the objectifying?' I asked."

"'The movement may have helped some, but it was a two-edged sword. The feminist undertaking led to women having multiple roles—employee, employer, mother, wife, homemaker, AND men's playthings. This is what the ideology wrought. At least, this has been the upshot in my opinion and experience.'"

"'Yikes. Delores, I didn't realize this is still

happening—post feminism's emergence,' I said."

"'Yes, Mark, women are still a man's wet dream. You should pay more attention, especially as a teacher of young people,' Delores said."

"Other than dreaming, are men still just after you for sex and not for you as a person?' I asked."

"'Mark, your naiveite is showing. The answer, unfortunately, is yes. However, when the fantasies are not realized, or the act not fulfilled as frequently as it once was, or the way men want it to transpire—then it is good-bye baby. You get the point now don't you Mark?' Delores asked."

"'Delores, I am trying to get it. Although, I may not be there yet,' I said concluding the conversation."

"Did the exchange with Delores end there?" Ana asked.

"Yes, Ana. As the discussion with Delores ended, the music grew even louder, clanging dinner dishes were cleared, and the dancing began. Delores had made her point—I finally figured out what she was trying to tell me."

"The point you figured out, Sweetheart, is…?"

"Ana, at first in this recounting you called me Honey, but later in this recital you have been calling me, Sweetheart."

"Yes. I did make the switch. The subject under discussion seems to warrant such a term of endearment—like Sweetheart."

"Oh, to continue then—when I was in high school, Ana, I fell into the sexualization of society at the time. I was a different person back then."

"Completely different?" Ana asked.

"No, not completely, but I have learned over the fifty years."

"Are you sure you have learned?"

"I think so."

"What have you learned, Sweetheart?"

"It sounds as if you might be questioning whether I have learned to regard women with the full respect you and other women deserve."

"Yes, my dear husband, that would be helpful for us to talk about," Ana asserted.

"How long do we have to discuss the subject?" I asked.

"As much time as we need—Sweetheart—and as much time as you need," Ana said.

Chapter 26: Bailey

In my life, I have had few close friends and acquaintances outside Bailey T. S. Memorial High School's faculty and students.

I have held my family closest to me—my wife, Ana—my son, Joel—my daughter, Suzie, and hopefully someday—grandchildren.

We, the Blenchards, have had until recently another member of our family—Bailey.

Bailey breathed life into the moments we spent with her. We loved this yellow Labrador totally, and she loved us fully in return.

For years, Bailey has been my meandering companion. In the time I have spent walking and talking with Bailey, we have relished nature's serenity. As we roamed, Bailey scampered ahead of me, pausing periodically to bask in the sunshine. She has wandered with me, played with me, sat with me, slept with me, and abides within me.

Bailey has lived for over ten years with me and my family. It has been a lifetime for her—not long enough for us.

We cried when Bailey chased squirrels to heaven.

Bailey left her paws on our hearts.

Chapter 27: Labor Day

School begins tomorrow.

It will be the first time in fifty years I will spend the day at home, not in a classroom.

Strange sensations trickle through me this Labor Day. I have had only one full-time job—teaching in Bailey High.

When I retired in June of 2020, the prospect of missing the first day of school did not unsettle me. I have my family, books yet to read, and have plenty to do around the house.

For decades, I have ogled household projects needing my attention. I have put the tasks on hold. I had to get ready for teaching in Bailey T. S. Memorial High School—my life's vocation as well as my avocation.

In 1970, after the Gorham, Massachusetts, school district offered me a position, I wondered how difficult teaching could be. Teaching for half a century has led me to discover that teaching is as difficult as it is exhilarating.

Since I was five years old, I have been in school classrooms from kindergarten through college. I know little else, nor have I wanted to do anything else. I have loved everything about teaching—getting ready for class, working with students, thinking about each day.

There is a pit roiling my stomach today. I am spending Labor Day without anticipating seeing my colleagues and students on the first day of school.

Instead of facing students on Tuesday, I will be eyeing my home's walls.

School is yet to begin. I ache for a room with chairs, tables, students—noise.

I have contemplated revoking my retirement but realize that is not wise even if it were possible. I could substitute teach or maybe even be a long-term sub. After thinking about it, I dismissed the idea of returning to Bailey High even part-time. I made my decision to retire—I will stick with it.

I have read and heard that the first month of retirement is invigorating. It was for me to a point. I had no papers to grade, and I did not have to be in an appointed place each hour. Soon, the euphoria vanished.

In retrospect, being in a place at a specific time to do something important is bliss to me.

I do have things to do—read, meet with friends, love my family, catch up on correspondence, discuss current issues with the Saturday group, and tackle endless chores.

I long to gaze into my classroom again. I crave the laughter, the shuffling furniture, the bantering—the clamor.

As this autumn looms, sleep dwells.

Chapter 28: Quest

"Dear Faculty and Students: March 19, 2021

I write to you about my husband.

Mark Blenchard taught in Bailey T. S. Memorial High School for fifty years. He loved teaching and working with you—his students and colleagues.

As you know by now, Mr. M. died four days ago. A months long bout with Coronavirus-19 left Mark's immune system and general health compromised. Had a vaccine been available in time to prevent an infection, Mark said he would not have 'cut in line.' He said, 'I will wait my turn.' My husband would rather die first before he took advantage over others. He had spent his life defying special privilege.

Mark quarantined himself in our basement away from his family and friends. We shared meals and time together, but at a safe distance. Even though my husband and I were separate physically, our souls continued to enmesh and exist as one.

When the virus dissipated and his condition improved, Mark came back to his family. Although he kept his physical distance, his love caressed us.

The virus, however, had taken its toll.

I will return home with him in a day or so. When I

arrive in Gorham, my family will plan and prepare for virtual memorial services.

My husband's body will be cremated which was his wish. He asked previously that when he passed that an urn with his ashes be placed as near the high school as the board of education will permit.

When Mark retired, I believe he left half his heart in the school. The rest of his heart remained with his family. Mark faithfully loved me and his children. He hoped someday he would have grandchildren.

Mark, as my lifelong husband and partner (such wonderful words—husband, partner, wife…) had not been feeling well recently, but he did not want to put off the trip to Canada. He wanted to find any trace he could of his family and heritage. He told me he had put it off for too long. We only made it as far as Maine.

After he retired, I could see being without a classroom in which to teach left a gap in Mark's soul. Mark taught in his sleep. He frequently told me throughout the years that he dreamed about classes he planned to teach. Mark thought about teaching during his twenty-four hours every day—365 days each year.

My intensely human life-partner had his foibles. Mark spent his life trying to grow as a person and educator. In his mind, he never became the teacher he sought to be. To those of us who knew and loved him, Mr. M. exemplified the teacher as learner. He was still *becoming* as he reached toward his last breath.

I loved the precious moments with my husband. He was the center of my life and still is. We have devoted our lives to each other and our family. Mark lived a meaningful life in his seventy-two years. He cherished the precious time spent with his family, his colleagues, and his students.

We were in Ellsworth, Maine when Mark died. We

were unsuccessful in our search for Mark's roots and birthright. Mark was disappointed we could not track his legacy. I, also, have not been able to find mine.

After the physician at the hospital determined Mark had passed, I called our children. Joel and Suzie assured me they would continue the search for their parents' ancestors. Our children have loved me and Mark totally. This love has brought great comfort to their mother and father.

Upon retirement, Mark calculated he had taught at least 100 students per year, equaling 5,000 over his fifty-year teaching career. Many more students passed Mr. M. in Bailey High's corridors and thought of him as their teacher.

Mark retired on June 15, 2020. He died some nine months to the day after his retirement.

We loved each other.

I miss him.

Respectfully, Ana Blenchard

P. S. The Gorham, Massachusetts, school system has activated Mark's email address so those who wish to do so can send an email our family will receive."

In the thirty days after Mark Blenchard's email account reopened, students and citizens from within and beyond Gorham's borders sent 8,963 reminiscences to Mr. M.'s family. Some of the messages were from Mark's students, some from students who attended Bailey T. S. Memorial High School but did not have him as their classroom teacher, some from Gorham's citizens, and some from admirers who had heard about the teacher who had taught for half a century in Bailey High.

Chapter 29: Independence

On the last day of school in June of 2021, the Board of Education in the town of Gorham, Massachusetts, announced, "Mark Blenchard's ashes have been set in an urn and buried in a flower bed adjacent to the school he taught in for fifty years. A granite stone upon which the teacher's name has been engraved signifies the spot where the urn has been placed."

The Gorham Police Department reported on the Fourth of July that they found an unlocked door at Bailey T. S. Memorial High School. The report further indicated, "Mr. M.'s urn containing his ashes has been removed from the flower bed outside the school. The stone marker with Mark Blenchard's name imprinted remains."

A note left at the burial site specified:

"The buried urn with Mr. M. in it has been carefully and reverently retrieved from the flower bed and positioned in the school building. Henceforth, Mr. M. will forever be in the school he loved. If you look for the urn, you will not find it. We, his former students, know how to care for Mr. M. and his legacy. We believe teachers live forever in their students' hearts and minds."

The message was signed, "The Students, Colleagues, Parents, and Friends of our Teacher—Mark Blenchard—Mr. M."

A postscript noted, "Mr. M's urn resides in the school next to another recovered urn. The adjoining urn is inscribed, 'Mr. K., esteemed Teacher in Bailey T. S. Memorial High School, 1960 to 1985.'"

Chapter 30: Epilogue

On September 1, 2021, the Gorham Police Department announced it had completed the investigation into an incident that occurred at Bailey T. S. Memorial High School in the summer of 2021.

In an interview with the *Gorham Daily News*, Police Chief Ricky Brezos reported: "No arrests have been made in the case of the unlocked door at the high school which was discovered on Independence Day. In addition, the investigation has been closed regarding the removal of an urn containing Mark Blenchard's ashes along with an urn containing Ken Lewiston's remains."

The following notice appeared in the Daily News on December 19, 2021:

"A baby boy weighing 7 pounds and 6 ounces joined our community yesterday. He is the child of Robert Allen Marino and Suzie Blenchard Marino. The newborn, Mark Blenchard Marino, has been named after his maternal grandfather. Gorham's newest resident and his parents are doing well. The baby's grandmother, Ana Blenchard, who lives at 60 School Street, is at the hospital with her grandson.

"Ms. Blenchard said, 'I shall take care of my grandchild after his parents return to work. Prior to being able to walk and understand on his own, I plan to wheel the carriage carrying my grandbaby around Bailey High. I will tell little Mark about his grandfather, Mr. M., and the tale of the two urns.'"

JOHN SPLAINE *has taught for over fifty years at the high school and college level. He taught in high schools in Maryland and New Hampshire, and taught in colleges in Colorado, Maryland, New Hampshire, and West Virginia. Splaine has written nonfiction books in government, history, and media literacy.*

www.ingramcontent.com/pod-product-compliance
Lightning Source LLC
Chambersburg PA
CBHW020324260626
47156CB00004B/1370

* 9 7 8 1 9 5 0 3 8 1 8 3 8 *